MEDITERRANEAN ADVENTURE

MEDITERRANEAN ADVENTURE

PAT PHILLIPS

G.K. Hall & Co. • Chivers Press
Thorndike, Maine   Bath, England

This Large Print edition is published by G.K. Hall & Co., USA and by Chivers Press, England.

Published in 1999 in the U.S. by arrangement with Maureen Moran Agency.

Published in 1999 in the U.K. by arrangement with the author.

U.S. Softcover   0-7838-0414-8   (Paperback Series Edition)
U.K. Hardcover   0-7540-3628-6   (Chivers Large Print)
U.K. Softcover   0-7540-3629-4   (Camden Large Print)

The text of this Large Print edition is unabridged.
Other aspects of the book may vary from the original edition.

Set in 16 pt. Plantin.

Printed in the United States on permanent paper.

British Library Cataloguing in Publication Data available

Library of Congress Cataloging in Publication Data

Phillips, Pat.
    Mediterranean adventure / Pat Phillips.
      p. cm.
    ISBN 0-7838-0414-8 (lg. print : sc : alk. paper)
    1. Large type books. I. Title.
[PS3566.H498M44   1999]
813′.54—dc21   98-31302

MEDITERRANEAN ADVENTURE

Chapter 1

As the plane gained altitude the green fields of Ireland disappeared until all that Moira could see were choppy clouds. She leaned back against the orange upholstered seat. Though this holiday had been eagerly awaited, now that home was actually left behind she experienced a wave of panic. It was foolish to feel this way, she thought in anger, when this past month she had thought of little else but the preparations for this trip. Why spoil it by being afraid?

The answer to that question was easy: she had never been away from home by herself. This Italian holiday was meant to be an adventure, but she had not intended to take it alone. Elspeth should have been beside her, eager to greet new challenges with a reckless smile and a characteristic toss of her auburn hair.

With a sigh Moira looked down at the snow-fields of cloud, wondering if Heaven was hidden behind them. Heaven . . . Elspeth would have laughed at that, for she had considered herself far from saintly. She had always said she would definitely go the other way when the time came. It had come unexpectedly last winter, when Moira's cousin had fallen to her death in a freak accident in the Italian Alps.

Elspeth Breen, a successful model, had been on an assignment to model a collection of ski wear for the Italian designer Sergio Campella. A carefree ride in a ski lift had turned to tragedy when the car became uncoupled and plummeted to the icy slopes below. Elspeth had never regained consciousness.

Moira found it difficult to believe that her cousin was dead. At the newsstands glossy closeups of Elspeth's famous profile had captured her attention: those large hazel eyes, outlined exotically in purple or green, her dazzling smile that seemed to say, "Come on, Moira, don't be afraid, take a chance. . . ."

For as long as she could remember, Moira had followed Elspeth's lead. At the convent school they had attended, Elspeth had been the scourge of the district, invariably leading her less courageous cousin into dozens of scrapes. Moira was forced to smile when she pictured Sister Bernadette chastising them, trying to maintain a stern expression — though Elspeth's pleading, tear-filled eyes could melt the coldest heart.

Moira was not as fortunate as Elspeth where looks were concerned. While her cousin had been tall and willowy, Moira considered herself short and dumpy. Instead of beautiful auburn, her hair was medium brown tinged with red. Instead of a luxuriant supply of waves and curls, Moira had thin, straight hair, plaited in pigtails. And where Elspeth's dusting of freckles had been attractive, poor Moira viewed her own brown-spattered complexion with despair. On her squat nose freckles were ugly, while Elspeth's well-known profile had been enhanced by the sun's kisses.

"Ugly duckling" was Moira's childhood name for herself. Now, thanks to maturity and a slimming diet from a women's magazine, her body was more slender. The freckles remained to taunt her, but all she could do was try to hide them with a covering make-up: "Guaranteed to cover unsightly blemishes and freckles," stated the label. Confidently Moira had brought the new cosmetic home, much to her father's disgust. Patting her face self-consciously, Moira smiled at a passing stewardess. She could not really blame Dad. In Castle Brennan it was still considered scandalous to wear eye shadow.

The reminder of home gave Moira a pang of homesickness. What a day it had been! Up in the cool, fragrant dawn, too excited to eat, then rattling over the country roads in Dad's ancient car, leading a happy procession. Almost the entire village had come to Shannon Airport to wave her on her way, with Mrs. Brennan, the surviving member of the local gentry, leading them. Sister Bernadette wished her a safe journey and gave her a rosary to remind her to say her prayers. Even Tim, the cowman from the farm over the hill, was there, a grin on his leathery face and a rose in his shabby jacket.

A daughter of the village going to Italy, even if it was only for a two-week holiday, was a great event. The last person to leave the village had been Tim's son, Gerald, who had gone to America two years ago. Before that it had been Elspeth. But the villagers had not been excited over her departure. "No good will come of it," they had prophesied. In a way they had been right. If Elspeth had stayed in Castle Brennan, she might have taught school or worked in the tobacconist's, the balmy, misty air preserving her lovely complexion. But Elspeth was ambitious, and when she was offered a chance to become a model, wild horses could not have kept her in the backward hamlet.

Since she was four Elspeth had been Moira's constant companion. They had grown as close as sisters after the death of Elspeth's parents in a car crash. Loneliness had forced Moira to pursue new interests to fill the void left by her cousin's departure. She had taken a typing course, and she had also learned to drive; both skills she later found invaluable in her job with the local estate agents.

When Elspeth's unexpected letter had come last December, Moira had been overjoyed. Her cousin had invited her to Italy to spend two weeks in Santa Maria, a small resort on the Adriatic Sea. For Elspeth it would be combining business with pleasure, but for Moira it would be two weeks of enchantment, made doubly exciting by the international fashion show in which Elspeth would wear some of the most glamorous clothes in the world.

"Don't worry about the cost, darling — I know the proprietor. We get a tremendous discount. Perhaps you'll meet a millionaire and be rich for the rest of your life. One thing, though, the conte who owns the castello is mine. He's absolutely divine. You remember the designer I was telling you about — Sergio? Well, darling, the conte's his elder brother. I have to rush as usual. Say the word and I'll book you.

Love, Elspeth"

Moira had unconsciously taken the worn letter from her purse, and, though she practically knew its contents by heart, she reread the invitation in violet ink in Elspeth's spidery handwriting. It did not seem right to be going to Santa Maria without her, though Elspeth would have wanted it that way. Mum and Dad had insisted that Moira go through with the proposed holiday, thriftily reminding her that the money was already paid, but really not wanting her to miss the chance of a lifetime. She could not help wondering uneasily what the conte would think of her arrival so soon after Elspeth's death. Would he be angry, or merely treat her with indifference?

Winding her handkerchief nervously in her hands, Moira bit the pink lipstick from her mouth. If she could have done it this morning, she would have turned back. But instead she had to be brave and smile, pretending that she was looking forward to this adventure, when inside she was really scared to death.

"Would you like a magazine, Miss Connor?"

Moira found a stewardess leaning across the seat beside her, proffering a magazine. Politely she accepted, though she did not really want to read. Nervousness interfered with her concentration. Soon Moira was agonizing over all the obstacles that faced her. She could not speak Italian, and there would be no one there to help her. Even the thought of going through customs was frightening. After that ordeal she would have to find the bus to Santa Maria, then a taxi to the castello. Surely everyone knew where Hotel Castello was; Elspeth had said it was famous for miles. But what if no one had heard of it?

Two hours later, hot and tired but triumphant, Moira stood in the wide square of a bustling Italian town with an unpronounceable name. Customs had been an ordeal. Though it could never have been as bad as she had imagined, the language barrier had slowed her down. Disorganized as usual, Moira was embarrassed to find her passport buried at the bottom of her flight bag. She produced an array of toiletries, much to the amusement of the grinning customs officer, who curiously examined her lotions and creams. With scarlet cheeks she finally found her passport. To add to her frustration, the items would not fit back into the flight bag. It took the assistance of two customs men before Moira was ready to leave the airport.

Glancing at the strangers in the square, Moira sighed with relief. At a time like this, being unknown did have its advantages. How humiliating it would have been to be with people from home who would never allow her to forget the spectacle she had made of herself!

"Is this the stop for the bus to Santa Maria?" she asked pleasantly, approaching a woman holding a basket of vegetables.

The woman smiled broadly, her mouth ugly with blackened teeth. "No English," she explained, still smiling.

"I'm very sorry," Moira apologized, retreating to survey the other passengers. Elspeth would have smiled and asked, "Does anyone speak English?" Why didn't she do that? At worst they would only ignore her, and she might find a willing translator.

A cream-colored bus sped around the corner of the buildings, scattering shoppers and pigeons alike. With a squeal of brakes, the vehicle stopped. Before Moira could voice her new question, she was elbowed out of the way as the noisy crowd boarded the bus. The movement was so rapid that she was left clutching her flight bag and gasping with surprise.

"This bus you want, signorina?" the driver sang, poking his bronzed face through the open window.

"Well, I . . . I'm not sure, I . . ." Moira faltered, reaching into her purse for the brochure from the hotel.

"Santa Maria and any place on the way," he said helpfully.

"Oh, this is it, then," Moira cried in relief, trying to juggle her suitcases toward the bus, which seemed poised on the point of departure. The engine roared, the sound accompanied by a chorus of pings, while the smell of oil from the motor lay heavy in the afternoon heat.

The bus driver bounded to her side, easily hefting her cases aboard. When his hand shot out immediately for a tip, Moira willingly paid, glad to have his assistance. Pocketing the change, he winked, his sweeping glance appreciative.

"Do you go as far as Hotel Castello?" she asked, avoiding his bold brown eyes.

"*Si.*"

In a moment the bus was lurching forward, sending Moira into the bulging arms of a large peasant woman in the front seat. Apologizing as she helped retrieve cheeses and stalks of asparagus, Moira grabbed the edge of the seat to keep her balance. Feeling as if she were aboard a fishing boat in a storm, she stepped carefully toward an empty seat at the rear of the bus. Moira was so glad to sit down at last that she overlooked the limp neck of a plucked fowl dangling from a wicker basket on the seat beside her. Even the pungent odor of Gorgonzola cheese exuding from the basket could be overlooked for the moment. All that mattered was the bliss of a place to sit and the comforting knowledge that she was on the last leg of her journey.

The bus lurched along country roads, passing fields and farmhouses, slowing only when a village blocked the route. At first Moira tried to steady herself at each bounce, but she eventually gave up trying. Her intention had been to doze on the journey, though she now realized that sleep would be impossible, for resting her head against the window frame only intensified the jolts.

"Some ride, huh?" a girl exclaimed from the opposite seat.

Relief washed over Moira at the sound of an American accent. Thank goodness there was another person aboard the bus who spoke English. She could have kissed the stranger with joy.

"You don't know how terribly glad I am to see you," Moira gasped, catching wildly at the seat to avoid being dumped in the aisle.

"Tracey Cole, at your service, friendly interpreter at reasonable prices!" The girl laughed, extending her hand.

Moira seized the suntanned hand, enviously conscious of Tracey Cole's beautiful fingernails, polished in pearlized pink.

"I'm Moira Connor."

"English?"

"Almost. I'm Irish."

"Say, you surprise me; none of that thick brogue."

"Sorry to disappoint you," Moira apologized, trying to smooth her hair into place. Tracey Cole made her freshly aware of her own disheveled appearance. The other girl looked as if she had just stepped out of a beauty salon, with her ash-blonde hair, sleekly brushed in a long pageboy, curving at shoulder length. The style complimented her classic features. Tracey's skin was honey tan — with no trace of a freckle, Moira discovered with fresh envy. Some people had all the luck!

"I'll get over it," Tracey quipped, reaching in her purse for a cigarette. "Want one?"

Moira declined the offer, and Tracey lit her own cigarette with a jeweled lighter. "You're smart. Smoking's a bad habit."

"They didn't allow smoking at the convent. I suppose I just never started," Moira explained, uncomfortably feeling as if she owed an apology. At the mention of a convent, Tracey's perfect brows raised a notch, but she did not comment.

"How long are you staying in Santa Maria?"

"Two weeks. Are you staying there as well?"

"Sure, it's the only decent town for miles," Tracey replied with a grimace. "I'm not hung up on all this rustic living. I prefer a bit of luxury on my vacation."

Moira laughed, hardly surprised by the statement. Tracey looked as though she were used to the lap of luxury. Her white tailored dress was still immaculate. And the sandals on her narrow feet were not from a low-priced chain store. It would be a coincidence if Tracey were staying at the castello, too.

16

"You're not staying at Hotel Castello, are you?"

"Right again. That where you're headed?"

"Yes."

Though she had to be quick to catch it, Moira could not help noticing the surprise that registered on Tracey's face. Uncomfortably she realized that it was probably not the coincidence, but rather that someone so ordinary would stay at a luxury hotel.

Tracey talked about her family in Maine, where her father held a position with an investment firm, while her mother enjoyed the demanding role of clubwoman of the year.

"They'll never miss me. I guess it was a relief when I went to college — took me out of their hair, so to speak," Tracey finished in her cool, low voice. "I'm going to Rome as an interpreter when this vacation's over."

Moira exclaimed over the exciting prospect of the job. She had discovered that by now they were almost alone on the bus. The remaining passengers were suntanned farm women carrying bulging straw baskets of provisions. All the other travelers had alighted at farms and villages on the way.

"We'll be there in a couple of minutes," Tracey revealed, dabbing her already immaculate nose with a powder puff.

Frantically Moira tried to tidy her appearance. When she arrived at the hotel it would be doubly humiliating to look as if she had come through a whirlwind. Along with the dust of travel she wiped away the last vestige of her freckle-covering make-up, now only a grimy orange patch on her handkerchief.

At last the final corner of the twisting road was rounded, and there, shimmering in the afternoon sun, was Hotel Castello.

The castello was immense. Though Moira had seen many of the Norman castles of Britain, this fortress of solid rock seemed more like a picture from a fairy tale. Jutting gables and small turrets capped by fluttering pennants reminded her of Sleeping Beauty's castle. Windows had been set in former arrow slits, and a hundred panes, winking like diamonds, caught the dazzling sunlight. Towering on a rise of ground, the castello dominated several acres of beautifully landscaped gardens. Though lovely in their terraced perfection, Moira found the gardens out of place. It was as if someone had fitted the pieces of a jigsaw puzzle, totally mismatching this grim medieval fortification to the parklike setting.

As the bus toiled up the steep incline, Moira admired the clipped grass and symmetrical rocky paths upon which spilled a profusion of multicolored, low-growing flowers, neatly restrained in pincushions of purple and yellow, blue and white. In the distance she glimpsed another garden, more wild and natural, where flowers tumbled among thickly matted walls of honeysuckle surrounding a ruined building.

"Well, what do you think of it?" Tracey asked.
"It's so big!"

"You can say that again. If this place were full, they'd make a fortune."

Further conversation was prevented as the driver braked, lurching them forward as the dusty bus skidded to a halt. His sun-bronzed face one great, teeth-baring grin, he waved toward the castello. "Your destination, signorinas."

"Thanks for nothing," Tracey added in an undertone as Moira thanked the young driver for his trouble. Encouraged by her smile, he scrambled to assist with her cases.

As Moira stepped into the bright sunlight she wished that Tracey had not seen her shabby cases, for she suspected the other girl's luggage to be streamlined and luxurious, like the cream-colored sets she had admired in Limerick when she had purchased her traveling wardrobe. Unfortunately, new luggage was beyond her means, so Moira made do with her suitcases from boarding-school days.

Tracey took her in tow, issuing commands in flawless Italian to the bellboy who came to greet them. Moira was grateful for her new friend's help. But as Tracey was shown to her room, Moira found that she would have to cope with the ordeal of checking in alone.

Moira did not want to impose, but she wished Tracey had not left so soon. It would have been reassuring to have her support at the reception desk. Apprehension churned her stomach. Now was the moment she had dreaded most of all: the revelation of her identity.

"I'm Miss Moira Connor," she announced, forcing assurance, though she felt like crawling to the nearest corner.

The slight man behind the desk peered at the hotel ledger over the top of his rimless glasses.

"I don't believe, signorina . . ." he began, his voice puzzled.

"I have a reservation booked in December," Moira said helpfully, wishing he could have simply found her name and sent her to her room without going into details.

"Connor," the man repeated, turning to the back of the book.

The minutes ticked by, and overhead a fan whirred noisily in the sultry afternoon heat. At last the man closed his book, an apologetic smile on his face. "Ah, yes, you are with the Campella collection. We did not expect the party till Wednesday."

"You mean I don't have a room?"

"I did not say that. Only that we did not expect you till Wednesday," he explained, his smile fading. "Fortunately your room is unoccupied at the moment."

Breathing a sigh of relief, Moira took the key he handed her. "I'm sorry. I didn't know I was included in the Campella party."

That the man was not listening was obvious by his answer. "It is not my fault," he grumbled. "I am not usually at the desk. Have a pleasant stay, signorina."

Glad to escape, Moira hurried toward the elevator. What a marvelous stroke of luck! Now she could relax and enjoy her holiday. No one need know that she was Elspeth's cousin. With the fashion show opening in a few days, it was doubtful whether anyone would bother to check her reservation to find out who she was. This way she was just another tourist. The weight of apprehension lifted from her shoulders, Moira hummed a catchy tune as the elevator soared upward.

Chapter 2

Moira woke the next morning to the unfamiliar sounds of the hotel. For a moment she was puzzled by her surroundings. The blue satin cover on the bed, the matching swag curtains with the heavy gold fringe, even the room itself, were unknown. Half-rising from her pillow in alarm, Moira sank back in contentment as she remembered. This was the first morning of her adventure.

Stretching in the luxury of the bed, Moira admired the lofty ceiling with its molded-plaster design picked out in gold leaf. The walls were pale cream with blue satin panels, and though from here they looked marvelous, last night Moira had noticed the careful mending of the worn material. Even the weighted bottom of the beautiful curtains was frayed. It was sad to allow such a lovely place to run down.

There was a knock on the door, and a maid crept inside. The girl placed a silver tray on the bedside table before stealing out again, thinking Moira was still asleep.

Moira gave no sign of recognition, still unsure of herself in these luxurious surroundings. It was the same lack of confidence that had forced her to eat in her room last night. After the tiring journey she felt too weary to face the elegant people she had glimpsed going down to dinner. Tonight, she told herself, sitting up in bed, tonight I will go downstairs. But dinner time was a comforting eternity away. First she was going to explore the sights. There was no better way to begin the day than with one of those rolls, wafting fresh-baked fragrance from the tray beside the bed.

After eating the Continental breakfast of rolls and coffee, Moira dressed hurriedly, anxious to see the town. For her first day of sight-seeing she wore her lime-green linen suit. The slim style made her look elegant, and pausing before the mirror, Moira drew her shoulders back, pulling herself to maximum height. Against the green her hair looked red, she thought with pleasure, giving the loose strands a final pat.

Outside, the air was still cool. There was none of the oppressive heat that she had encountered yesterday. The walk from the castello was tiring, and Moira was thankful she had chosen sandals instead of her more fashionable high-heeled pumps.

Though it was early, Santa Maria bustled with life, the open market overflowing with noise and color. Fruit, brilliant in the morning sun, spilled bounteously from wooden stalls. Purple and green grapes, oranges and apples, bananas and enormous green melons rested side by side on the crude stalls. As she passed, vendors eagerly held up bunches of grapes to her, praising them in extravagant Italian, extolling the virtue of the fruit. Shyly Moira shook her head, walking on, to their disappointment; or to trained eyes the formality of her dress immediately spelled "tourist."

The townspeople were casual in their attire. Moira realized that she was probably the only woman who was not bare-legged. The local women wore mostly black garments, creating a monotone against the sallowness of their skin. Children ran around half-naked, fighting for discarded fruit among the rickety wooden legs of the market stalls. The sun-bronzed men wore undershirts, while several of the younger vendors were bare-cheated, gold religious medals gleaming brightly from the black hair on their chests.

It was a laughing throng, bickering good-naturedly, taunts sprinkled with profanities that were taken in good spirit. Moira was struck by the happiness of the children toddling at their mothers' sides. She was also slightly embarrassed to see women openly nursing their babies, a sight alien to her reserved British upbringing.

Conscious of the dawning blush on her cheeks, Moira turned from the marketplace, walking swiftly over the cobbled square where multicolored pigeons strutted in the morning sun. White tables and chairs from the cafes spilled into the piazza, but it was still too early for many customers. Lounging beneath a red striped umbrella were a couple of young men who eyed her with open approval, bringing the blood back stingingly to her face. On the first day of her visit to Italy, Moira was made aware of the earthiness of the Italian nature. They openly showed emotions she had been taught to conceal and publicly appreciated things she had always thought should be private.

Holding her head high, she entered the cool shadow of the narrow street leading to the rocky beach. Here tall buildings pressed close, leaving only a narrow ribbon of blue sky overhead. Bright red geraniums spilled from baskets on the balconies, the flowers mingling with strings of laundry slung haphazardly from upstairs windows. Even here there was noise. Babies played in the shadow of the buildings, their cries mingling with the laughter and voices filtering from behind the closed doors of houses. Women sang as they scrubbed doorsteps, while from an upper story a man's voice warbled an impassioned rendition of "O Sole Mio."

The tang of the sea was in Moira's nostrils. Before her spread the gleaming whiteness of the seawall, where amber nets were strung, drying against the rock. From behind the wall echoed the steady roll of the ocean. Here the odor of fish mingled with the smell of oil from the boats.

Pausing, Moira turned her back on the Adriatic to survey the little town stretching steeply uphill behind her, crowned by the castello, toylike from this distance. Everywhere was a jumble of color, sun-faded and mellow, yet contrasting brilliantly with the bright blue sky. The day was superbly clear, the air thin and light, washing everything with a certain luminosity similar to an Italian-landscape painting in a museum. It was all so different and exciting. Moira breathed deeply, drawing in the pulsing life of it all, and she sighed with pleasure, finding it almost unbelievable that she was here at last.

By afternoon the prospect of the uphill trek to the hotel was unappealing. Moira had walked blisters on her heels exploring the twisting alleys and huddled streets of Santa Maria. Close to the dock some of the streets were impassable to vehicles, their surface nothing more than a series of steps rising steeply toward the church. Every street seemed to converge on the piazza, jutting at odd angles to achieve this goal, but coming out eventually on the broad, flagged square. The piazza was the hub of life, housing the open market, the cafes, and the beautiful church. For Moira it was an exciting preview of Italy. In the incense-sweet darkness of the church of Santa Maria, adorned by magnificent murals and aglow with flickering points of light, she felt sure that this was one of the loveliest towns in the country.

Unprepared for siesta time, Moira found herself abandoned beneath the striped awnings of a cafe, left to sip the remnants of her cool drink. Only the pigeons remained, pecking among the gray paving stones, until at last even they disappeared, seeking cooler roosts as the afternoon heat shimmered across the square.

Feeling completely alone, Moira stretched her tired legs and wondered what to do. She squinted against the intensity of the sun to see the time on the clock across the piazza. The elongated shadow of the campanile extended dark fingers over her chair for a while as the sun rose higher, but soon even this comforting coolness was gone. It was too hot to walk back to the castello, so she would have to wait till siesta was over, however long that might be.

An hour had passed. By now Moira felt uncomfortably sticky. A small patch of shadow was available in the angle of the buildings, and she moved her white cafe chair to make use of the shade. Now that she had taken off her shoes, her hot feet felt a little better, but she would have loved to dangle them in the beckoning water of the town fountain. The sound of running water taunted her as she looked longingly at the splashing basin with its chipped Neptune and frolicking mermaids.

"I knew it. Come on."

Moira found Tracey Cole beside her. "How did you know I was here?"

"It figured." Tracey laughed, but her face was kind. "Only a poor innocent like you would sit outside in the heat."

"I didn't realize everything closed in the afternoon," Moira explained sheepishly, putting on her shoes and fastening the buckles.

"That's okay. Next time you'll remember."

Tracey grinned as she picked up Moira's handbag. "At least you didn't haul that brown overnight case around with you."

Feeling silly, Moira took her white purse. Tracey did not know that she had almost brought the brown one. After all, it was new and quite expensive, but even before she left the hotel the weight had been too much.

"Are you on foot?" she asked.

"Me? You should know me better than that! I've got a car over there," Tracey said, leading the way.

A flame-red sports car was parked in front of the Santa Maria post office. Tracey opened the door, ushering Moira inside. The top was down and the sun had made the leather seats hot. With a muffled "Ouch!" Moira slid carefully over the soft upholstery.

"Is this your car?" she asked as Tracey turned the key in the ignition.

"No. I borrowed it from a friend. He's the kind of boy friend *you* need — a useful one!" She laughed, deftly backing the car down the narrow street. "Although you probably don't even drive."

"Yes, I do." The surprise that flickered across Tracey's classic features was a reward in itself.

In a few minutes they were back at the hotel. Today, Moira realized, she was even more grateful to see the castello than she had been yesterday. Thanking Tracey for her thoughtfulness, Moira went indoors, watching the other girl

28

speed away until the small red car was little more than a bright speck moving along the coast road.

At the castello dinner was served late. Long before the deep-voiced gong sounded in the dining hall, Moira was ravenously hungry.

What to wear for such a grand affair was the burning question. Her green linen suit was too much like daytime attire; besides, the spurting melon she had eaten for lunch at a wayside fruit stand had spotted the sleeves. Yet her pink chiffon dance dress was too fussy. At last she decided on the yellow linen that Elspeth had discarded last summer. It was embroidered down the sides in two wide panels of white daisies, and with her enamel daisy earrings the outfit should be attractive; it was dressy enough for the Falcon in Castle Brennan, but for Hotel Castello she was not sure.

Nervously Moira crept into the gloomy passage outside her door. The lanterns on the walls had been lit, and wavering orange light flickered in ghostly shadows about the rough stone. A middle-aged couple passed her at the top of the stairs, and they nodded politely. Moira's heart pitched with dismay. The lady was actually wearing diamonds, glittering and winking rainbows of color around the neck of her dark satin gown.

Below, in the massive hall, the dining table was beautifully laid with silver and crystal. Banks of scarlet flowers were massed in the center, as elaborate as any royal banquet.

With half a mind to turn back, Moira hesitated on the first step, feeling out of place in her casual attire. Perhaps she could say she had a headache tonight . . . but what about tomorrow and the next night?

The muted thud of footsteps sounded behind her, and just as she decided to race back to the safety of her room, a man said, "Good evening, signorina."

He came from the shadows, his hand extended. A heavy, jeweled ring glinted in the subdued light, making a large crest visible in the gold. Moira fastened her eyes on the ring, too self-conscious to look at its owner.

"Good evening," she replied politely, turning to leave.

"Have you forgotten something, signorina? Allow me to bring it for you," the man offered, stepping closer as she turned away.

"It's just my handkerchief," she mumbled lamely, feeling very foolish.

"Here, signorina, you may use mine."

Blocking her exit, he handed her a folded white handkerchief. Embroidered in the corner was the same crest she had noticed on the ring: a helmeted knight. The insignia was vaguely familiar, but in her current embarrassment Moira could not place it.

"Th-thank you," she stuttered.

"My pleasure, signorina."

He came into the light, and for the first time she found the courage to look at him. The man was tall for an Italian. He was suntanned, his dark hair neatly groomed, though a stubborn curliness erupted in the glossy waves, destroying their perfection. As he flashed her a smile, his teeth were revealed, white and even, contrasting with the darkness of his skin. He was very handsome, yet when he smiled it was only with his mouth — almost as if a giant travel poster of a suave, continental man welcoming her to Italy had suddenly come alive.

"Come, let me escort you to dinner."

There was little Moira could do but accept his polite offer. Gulping, she took the proffered arm, tucking her hand lightly beneath the sleeve of his white dinner jacket. Trying to look composed, she glided slowly down the wide, shallow staircase, touching the treads with her patent leather shoes to locate the back of the stairs beneath the thick red carpet. That was the way it was done, though several times she sneaked a glance to see if she was putting her foot in the right place. How terrible it would be if she stumbled when she was being taken to dinner by this handsome man! If only Jenny Healy at the tobacconist's could see her now, she would be so envious. Jenny had almost swooned with delight when Moira had told her she was going to Italy for her holidays.

Wishing she could take a picture of this event to send to her friend, Moira realized they were at the bottom of the stairs. She also noticed that the other diners were watching her as they stood politely beside their chairs — almost as if they were waiting for her arrival. A flush crept to Moira's cheeks at the unaccustomed attention, and she held her head high, trying to act as if this were commonplace to her. The lady with the diamonds treated her to a frosty smile, turning to the man beside her to whisper something behind her hand.

Ushering Moira to her chair with a small bow, the Italian departed. A chorus of admiring voices greeted him, and he was quickly surrounded.

"Carlo, darling, I thought you were sailing."

Moira knew that voice, but tonight Tracey was a stranger. A towering arrangement of curls cascaded down her head, her sparkling hair ornaments glittering in the light from the gigantic chandelier above the table. Her chic dress was slippery black satin with a daring decolletage.

Self-consciously Moira smoothed the skirt of her own dress where it was wrinkling over the hips, trying to iron out the creases with her hand. The signal to be seated was given, and in unison the diners obeyed.

Before her stretched a formidable array of silverware. Moira tried to remember to start at the outside and work inward, repeating this formula to herself as a waiter approached with a tray of chilled melon slices in silver bowls.

Though the food appeared to be delicious, Moira did not enjoy hers and afterward was not sure what she had eaten. She was far too conscious of the knives and forks, the bowls and napkins, the goblets for wine and water. There were two weeks of this, she thought with dismay; surely by the end of that time she would be used to it.

They were served coffee in paper-thin demi-tasse cups of white china, with a beautiful hand-painted design of roses edged with gold. Moira was admiring the delicate cup when she found that the man who had brought her to dinner was staring intently at her. Two days in Italy had introduced her to that masculine stare — a bold, appraising glance from which she looked away in discomfort. But his expression was different, for it was mingled with curiosity, and there was a question in his eyes.

The other guests were leaving, each going to the head of the table where the man was, exchanging a few words before leaving the room. It was as if he were the host, Moira thought as she carefully put down her cup so as not to crack the china. It was so delicate that it seemed as if a puff of wind would have sent the cup dancing across the table.

"Simply marvelous, Conte, delightful."

The woman's words startled Moira, and she looked about with interest. Where was the conte? He was someone she both dreaded and looked forward to meeting at the same time. As the lady with the diamonds swept majestically toward the stairs, Moira realized that she had already met him. The man in the white jacket was *il Conte del Santa Maria!*

She exclaimed loudly with surprise, so that he looked up in question at the sound. They were alone at the table, and she saw that he was waiting for her to depart.

"Is something wrong, signorina?"

"No, not at all," she replied, pushing back her chair. As she dropped her crumpled napkin on her plate, Moira saw the family crest embroidered in the corner of the linen. What a fool she had been not to recognize the coat of arms on his ring! She had seen it many times before. The device was worked into the stained-glass windows in this hall; it fluttered from the flag standards on the turrets; it was carved on the paneling and embroidered on the coverlets.

The conte had risen, too, and now he came to her side. "Signorina Connor, is that right?" he asked, a puzzled frown on his brow as he studied her face.

"Yes," Moira agreed, the truth of her relationship to Elspeth on the tip of her tongue.

"Strange," he murmured, glancing at her hair, "you are like someone I knew once, but the name is wrong."

She smiled politely, inwardly guilty because she knew it was Elspeth he remembered. By not speaking out she had sealed forever the opportunity to tell him that Elspeth was her cousin. Still, perhaps it was as well; to be reminded of his dead fiancee would only cause pain. Now she had met him, it was easy to see why Elspeth had fallen for the conte. This castello would have appealed to

Moira even if the owner had been old and unattractive. But the combination of the castello and a man as handsome and charming as the conte would prove irresistible to a woman like Elspeth.

"Good evening, signorina. I trust your stay with us will be pleasant," he said, bowing formally over her hand as he raised it to his lips.

The gesture had been impersonal, and Moira was disappointed, for she had been ready to color their meeting with romance. Now she realized it had merely been politeness. In seeing that she was comfortable, the conte was only playing the host.

As Moira trailed upstairs to her room, she became aware of someone watching her from the shadows of the gallery surrounding the hall. When she looked around she saw the blur of the conte's white dinner jacket as he moved away. *He* had been watching her. The discovery was at once exciting and a little disturbing. She had not met the designer, Sergio, but she was sure he was not as attractive as the conte. No wonder Elspeth had switched affections in midstream when she saw Carlo. Looking at it from a mercenary viewpoint, which Moira had to admit Elspeth had probably done, Sergio had inherited neither the title nor the castello.

Tomorrow morning, Moira decided, would be perfect for her first swim; so before she went to bed she laid out her bathing suit. The deep blue nylon was dark against the white satin chair.

With a smile she compared the contrast to her own body, picturing her skin milky white against the fabric. But the chair did not have freckles or bulges or spots, she reminded herself with an impatient shrug, coming back to earth. What about that, my girl?

Practical once more, she went to the bathroom to rinse her underwear. After hanging her hose to drip over the bathtub, Moira wandered about the room. From below filtered the strains of an orchestra playing for dancing. She could have put on her dance dress and gone downstairs, but she was still overawed by this magnificent hotel. Perhaps next week she would have the courage to dance with the other guests.

The night air was fragrant with the scent of flowers from the gardens. Pushing open the tall windows, Moira stared in wonder at the midnight-blue sky, heavily studded with stars. What a beautiful night! This was the type of night that she had dreamed about — moonlit, star-sprinkled, with the sound of the sea and soaring violins in the background. In these dreams, however, she was not alone; a handsome man danced with her, and later they kissed beneath the stars, as in the films she had seen and the books she had read, dreaming of a shimmering, sunlit land while the winter wind blew fiercely from the Irish sea. Now that she was actually here nothing had changed. She was still Moira Connor, and she was still alone. With a sigh Moira plucked a blossom from the flowering vine trailing around the stone columns of the balustrade.

A woman's laughter sounded below as two figures came into view, walking toward the trees. The moon cast darkly elongated shapes across the lawn, the man overshadowing the girl as they embraced by the fountain. Moira's heart thudded as she wished herself inside the girl. But the excitement turned to dismay as the couple looked toward the balcony. They could not see her standing in the shadow, but she could see them, for the white moon cast a flood of light over the figures. They looked as if they were on a stage set, so fantasy-like was the surrounding garden. The man plucked a spray of flowers from the bush beside the fountain while the girl exclaimed with delight; then he kissed her again, quieting her voice. With a sickening tug at her heart Moira turned away, for the man was the conte and the girl, Tracey Cole.

Chapter 3

Each morning after breakfast the hotel guests were driven to the beach in a blue minibus. Today there were only two other would-be bathers: an old-maid schoolteacher from Bath, who had struck up an acquaintance with Moira this morning at the breakfast table, and Mrs. Wilburn Kay, a gushing American lady on vacation with her husband.

Feeling self-conscious beneath the bus driver's unabashed stare, Moira clutched her striped beach robe, hiding the revealing expanse of bare skin.

"Now, isn't this nice, we're all going to the same place," Mrs. Kay remarked in her chatty, overbearing manner as they drove toward town. "I do declare, this place is right out of a movie."

"Oh, yes, very picturesque," the schoolteacher agreed stiffly. She wanted to return to her book, but Mrs. Kay kept her talking.

Though she was several seats away, Moira was unwillingly drawn into the conversation. It would be a relief to be free, but how to dodge Mrs. Kay was a problem.

At the first opportunity Moira made her escape, though she felt guilty for doing so when she saw the schoolteacher trying so hard to be

polite while Mrs. Kay kept up her gushing observations. It could not be helped. Being talked to
death was all Moira needed to ruin the morning.

Slipping between the crowded market stalls,
she darted down one of the twisting streets she
had discovered yesterday. Her last glimpse of the
others revealed Mrs. Kay bending close to Miss
Cross's ear as she screeched over the market
bustle, while the schoolteacher looked about
helplessly, waiting for her young compatriot to
come to her rescue.

After a futile search for a secluded stretch of
beach, Moira settled for a handkerchief of clean
sand beside a jetty. The Santa Maria beach was a
disappointment. Where there were no tourists,
there were fishermen talking as they mended
their nets, an occupation that allowed them time
to observe the passing women. Their presence
made her uncomfortable, for she knew a female
alone was considered fair game. Before she
moved away she was convinced that the men
intended to approach her, though she could not
understand a word of their conversation.

Plodding past the oily deposit of many sea-
sons' fishing boats, she found a clean spot large
enough to spread her beach robe. Here, behind
the shield of a sloping wall, she was out of the
men's view. Taking a note pad and a pen from
her red striped beach bag, Moira began a letter
to her parents, telling them about her luxurious
room at Hotel Castello.

After thirty minutes of furious writing, her

inspiration ran out. There were five closely written pages filled with descriptions of the town and hotel. It would be easier to write to Jenny Healy because anything fascinated her, so starved was she for romance. Moira recounted her meeting with the conte, extolling his virtues until she had to smile at her extravagance. What she did not write was the fact that he was already involved with Tracey Cole and that Tracey was poised and sophisticated, the perfect companion for an Italian count.

The memory of that scene beside the fountain took her attention, and Moira put down her letter. If only it had been she who stood there so confident and beautiful, she whose lips joined his in the romantic moonglow, discovering what it was like to be kissed by a count. *Il Conte.* The hereditary title made him nearly as exalted as a king, the illusion made real by the homage of his subjects, the beautiful people of Hotel Castello. His ancestors, who had built the castle in the turbulent past, had ruled the surrounding country with absolute power. Even though it was all so long ago, there was still that inborn assurance in his lean face, the near arrogance of knowing your bloodline stretched back to the royal houses of Italy.

A dreamy smile suffused Moira's features, and she slithered down in the warm sand, closing her eyes against the bright blue glory of the sky. It was so easy to picture him astride a horse, his armor flashing like fire in the sun, colored plumes bobbing from his helmet as he rode to battle. She would have waited faithfully for him, tending her gardens and working tapestries, secure in his love. The dream picture was so lovely that she dwelled on it for several minutes, almost lulled to sleep by the waves as she dozed beneath the warmth of the sun. Lapping water provided theme music for her mental extravaganza, in which a thousand knights charged down the hillside, pennants streaming in the wind. They would rally in the piazza to be blessed by the village priest, who would pray to God for the safety of their leader, Carlo, *il Conte del Santa Maria.*

"Oh, I say, what luck. I thought I'd never find you. We Britishers should stick together, don't you think, dear?" a voice stated heartily.

Eyes jarred open in shock, Moira bumped back to reality to find the schoolteacher from Bath puffing from her exertion as she creaked down on the sand beside her.

For over an hour Miss Cross entertained Moira with the story of her stroke of fortune in winning this holiday in a contest. "Such luck, my dear. Why, I haven't a clue about sports. A one-in-a-million chance, and I won it!"

Moira murmured appropriate congratulations, but she was thankful when Miss Cross tired of her story and was content to read. In her way the teacher was almost as wearying as Mrs. Kay. Besides, while Miss Cross talked Moira could not journey to the past and re-create the

41

splendid story of Santa Maria — or, more accurately, its conte.

When they arrived back at the hotel in time to clean up for lunch, Moira almost expected to find the castello transformed to its former splendor, so vivid had been her dream. The conte was nowhere to be seen, a blessing for which she was grateful. Her dreams had been too romantically intimate for her to be able to face him at the moment.

Only as she was dressing, admiring her reflection in the mirror, did Moira stop to consider that her cousin had been engaged to him. The realization was like a bucket of ice water on her dreams. To compete against Tracey was bad enough, but to try to overcome memories of Elspeth was impossible.

Seated beside Moira at lunch was a strange young man in a brilliant purple sweater, his long brown hair curling to his shoulders. Miss Cross, who had occupied this corner of the table in the morning, was nowhere to be seen.

"Hi, I'm Chris Bern. You must be Moira. I'm a friend of Tracey's," he introduced himself after a few minutes' silence.

With a shy smile Moira nodded, warming to the friendly young American with the engaging smile. Chris was in his early twenties. Brilliant eyes in a warm shade of milky brown dominated his sallow, square-jawed face. Though his long hair was well styled and clean, Moira knew Dad would have scornfully dismissed him as a hippie.

Perhaps he was an artist or an actor, she thought, drawn to his expressive eyes.

"I'm working with the Campella collection," Chris volunteered, almost as if he read her mind, and he grinned at the flush that lit Moira's cheeks.

"That must be interesting," she mumbled, looking back to her soup. It was a green liquid with pieces of unidentifiable vegetables floating on top. The concoction was unappetizing, and she relinquished the untouched bowl to a passing waiter.

"It's a lot of fun. I'm studying stagecraft, but this is a change, the models and everything," Chris continued. "Guess you could call me Campella's Man Friday. Photography, lighting, the works. The show comes to a standstill without me," he announced without modesty, a twinkle in his eyes.

"How long have you worked for Mr. Campella?" Moira asked, wondering if by chance he had been with Sergio long enough to know Elspeth.

"About eighteen months. I plan to go back to college this fall. That's where I met Tracey, in case you're wondering."

"I thought it was something like that. You don't strike me as the sort of person Tracey would —" Moira stopped in confusion. She had begun to say "pick up," but that was rude.

"Yeah, she does come on like a million dollars." Chris laughed, understanding at once. "I expect the conte's more her speed. For all we know she's got her eye on a title, though from what I hear contessas have a pretty high turn-over."

"Oh, what do you mean?" Moira asked in surprise.

"Well, the last girl who had her eye on the conte ended up at the bottom of a ski lift. And one of the contessas supposedly drowned herself, but there've been a few dark hints to the contrary. Anyway, that's gruesome enough for me. I told old Tracey to be pretty darned careful."

"But the girl killed on the ski lift — that was an accident," Moira insisted, her heart thudding uncomfortably.

"Sure, what else could it have been?" he agreed, changing the subject. "Anyway, sweet-heart, don't spoil your lunch. Have some gnocchi. If you like cheese, it's great."

But Chris's joking words had robbed Moira of her appetite, and the steaming gnocchi went untouched on her plate. Should she tell him that Elspeth had been her cousin? Though she toyed with the idea, Chris changed the subject and she never got it out.

Perhaps it was just as well, Moira thought later, sitting in a lounge chair on the terrace, lazy in the warm sun. If she told Chris she was related to Elspeth, he would tell Sergio, and the cat would be out of the bag. After that lovely dream this morning, it was more than she could stand to have a scene with the conte and spoil it all.

From this terrace she could watch the preparations for the fashion show. This was the day the desk man had told her the Campella people would arrive. Chris Bern must have come on ahead, for he was the only stranger she had seen at lunch. After meeting him she almost felt part of the group, for he had been so friendly toward her. While not living up to her romantic dreams of chivalrous knights, like the conte, Chris was not unattractive, Moira decided as he waved to her from the doorway.

"Hey, the big man's coming any minute if you want to catch him," Chris informed her, stopping for a moment beside her chair.

"Sergio Campella?"

"That's the one. By the way, sweetheart, you'd better hide that red head under an umbrella. Wouldn't want you to burn."

No sooner said than done. Moira was flattered to have such adoring masculine attention, and she basked in the shade of the large beach umbrella as Chris charged away, trailing miles of light cord behind him.

A flurry of movement at the hotel entrance took her attention. Moving her chair for a better view, Moira caught her breath as the colorful procession unwound from the chartered bus. There were the models, tall, immaculately dressed women carrying leather hatboxes, while an assortment of behind-the-scenes workers pulled baskets and trunks from the luggage compartment of the bus.

A silver-gray limousine glided to a halt behind the bus, and the driver slid gracefully from beneath the wheel. A blond man of slight, wiry build, yet very straight in carriage, he strutted around the unloading party, fussy as a mother hen. Rapid-fire orders were issued, and the already harassed workers increased their pace, shouting directions to each other.

With a parting command the man strode toward the hotel entrance, not sparing a glance for the castello's impressive facade. The powder-blue material of his suit shimmered in the light with a metallic glint, a tribute to its designer; for despite the skintight cut, the clothing fitted without a wrinkle. There was no doubt as to his identity. This was Sergio. As unlike his brother in both stature and coloring as Moira could imagine, but there was still a striking similarity in their arrogant assurance, their inborn knowledge of birth and power.

In spite of the shade of the umbrella, Moira later discovered she was sunburned. Her nose was bright pink, rivaling the shiny glow on her forehead. Just think, in Italy three days and already out of action.

After dinner Moira felt too hot to move. She tossed her white stole across the foot of the bed. However lovingly Mum had knitted that lacy creation, it was meant for cool Irish summer evenings, not this sweltering Italian version of a summer night.

A breeze stirred from the open windows, drawing her outside where it was cooler. The balcony itself was narrow, with barely enough room for two people. Weathered stone crumbled amongst the trailing pink-flowering vines wound about the balustrade. It was from such a balcony that Juliet had dreamed of Romeo. Moira leaned against the wall. Tossing back her hair and arranging the draperies of her dance dress, she pretended to be the tragic heroine of the classic love story.

In a rush the lines of the balcony scene came back as she recalled the amateur production by the school dramatic society in which she had played a lady of the court. Secretly she had coveted the leading role but would never have had the courage to attempt such a difficult part. Now, getting into the spirit of the role, her voice rose as, arms outstretched, she declaimed the final lines of the impassioned speech.

"And for that name, which is no part of thee,
Take all myself."

From below came the rich, warm tones of a man's voice, replying in Romeo's words.

"I take thee at thy word:
Call me but love, and I'll be new baptized;
Henceforth I never will be Romeo."

Moira gripped the edge of the balcony, her

face growing hotter as the seconds passed. To think that someone had overheard her play-acting, that he was probably laughing at her, made her feel faint with embarrassment. Eventually, with scarlet face, she leaned over the balcony, wondering who he could be. A flagged terrace dotted with wrought-iron tables and chairs stretched below. There was no mistaking the owner of the mysterious voice, for only one person was there, a grin of amusement on his dark face. It was the conte.

"I . . . I . . ." Moira began, but her words died in confusion. It was bad enough to have been overheard, but for the man to be Carlo del Santa Maria was the ultimate humiliation. He must think she was an absolute fool.

With a lazy movement he clapped, his gesture only compounding her discomfort. *"Brava!"*

"I didn't know anyone was there," she explained, withdrawing behind her impenetrable shield of British reserve.

"That's obvious," he agreed. "Won't you join me, Juliet?"

"No, thank you, I'm just retiring," she said, hoping she sounded suitably remote.

"Now don't say that. I'm your host; you can't refuse my invitation. I shall expect you in about five minutes."

He returned to a ledger that he had been reading by the brilliant light coming through the windows, and picking up a pen, he began to write, completely ignoring her.

With a snort of indignation Moira marched inside, closing the window with a bang, hoping he heard. It was hotter than ever in the bedroom, but she would not have opened the windows for the world. Sitting on her bed with sweat trickling down her neck, Moira thought about the conte's invitation. Though he had laughed at her when he should have pretended he had not heard, he *was* very attractive. Maybe she could go down for a few minutes. What harm would that do? Besides, he was the most exciting man she had met so far, possibly the only one she would meet in her entire life.

"You're five minutes late," he said, not sparing her a glance as she came to his table.

"Does that cancel the invitation?" she demanded.

"On the contrary!" He laughed, putting down his pen. "Do join me; the wine is excellent."

He poured a glass from a crystal decanter on a nearby serving cart, then, while she sipped her drink, he returned to his work. The papers appeared to be accounts, and he frowned over them as he worked. Moira was able to study the conte at close quarters. Tonight that usual theatrical smile was gone, and he had removed his suit jacket, draping it carelessly on the back of his chair. Lines on his forehead deepened to furrows as he worked.

Suddenly the lights went out as servants made the rounds of the downstairs rooms. The terrace was plunged into darkness, relieved only by the gleam of moonlight, falling slanted over the stone paving, where it illuminated an urn of sweet-scented, night-blooming flowers.

"It looks as though my bookkeeping is over for the night," he announced, closing the ledger. Then, gathering some papers in a stack, he returned them to an envelope.

"I'm surprised you attend to your own books," Moira said.

"It's a question of money."

"Money! You shouldn't have any money worries with a beautiful place like this." She laughed, holding out her glass for the refill he offered, though she knew she should stop with the first glass.

"There you are wrong, little Juliet."

The reminder of the balcony incident brought the blood to her face, and Moira stared at her hands, wishing he had not mentioned it when she was trying hard to forget.

"Now are you going to turn coldly British toward me?" he teased, drumming his fingers on the tabletop.

Sheepishly she shook her head. "No, but I wish you wouldn't think about that. I felt so silly."

"You shouldn't. It isn't every day one of my lady guests quotes lines from Shakespeare, especially such romantic ones."

Moira grinned, swallowing her discomfort. "You really surprised me. I'd no idea there was a flesh-and-blood Romeo down there."

"I know — that's what made it so perfect." He laughed again, leaning back in his chair. "It's unfortunate we can't pretend that Juliet lived here. Santa Maria could use the extra tourists."

"Oh, no, if you had all those busloads of tourists, the town would be spoiled," Moira said in dismay. "Being quiet is part of its charm."

"You have a point," he agreed, refilling his glass; and, instead of refusing more wine, Moira allowed him to pour her another. "I have visions of all those tourist millions coming in, so I have a slightly different viewpoint."

"But your lovely home, your birthright —" she began enthusiastically, not expecting his frown.

"My birthright," he repeated, an edge to his voice. "Oh, yes, how often I have been reminded of that!"

"Don't you like the castello?"

"Yes, as a home I suppose I have some affection for it; the castello is all I've ever had."

"It's wonderful enough for me. I'd be content," Moira enthused, the wine erasing her usual shyness. "You're lucky."

He smiled, studying her glowing face. "And you are nice."

"Thank you. Lucky and nice. We make a good combination."

There was no scorn to his grin. "I think, poor Juliet, that you've suffered an abundance of both sunshine and wine."

Instead of being offended, Moira smiled. She felt wonderful. The stars were brighter than any she had ever seen, the flowers more fragrant than she had believed possible.

"That's what Italy is famous for, isn't it?"

"Correct. And hospitality is also one of our virtues, especially where lovely young ladies are concerned. Will you allow me to show you my castello — a private tour not on the itinerary?" he asked, leaning closer while he gingerly tapped her scarlet nose with his finger. "We will also get some salve for your wounds."

"I'd love to," Moira gasped, wondering if he had really asked that question or if the wine had played tricks on her senses.

"Wonderful. I'll meet you in the lobby tomorrow after siesta. I am looking forward to it."

Chapter 4

Time crawled by, until the afternoon seemed endless. Moira was so excited by the anticipation of a romantic encounter with the conte that her hands shook as she held the book she was attempting to read. At last she gave up the effort, finding the prospect of her own romance more interesting than the adventures of the heroine in the novel.

Perhaps he had only been joking about meeting her this afternoon, she thought in horror as she began to pace the floor. Checking her watch, she found it was already two o'clock; not long now before she would discover if he had actually been serious about their date.

All day Moira had relived their conversation on the terrace to the exclusion of all else. Both Miss Cross and Mrs. Kay had looked daggers at her during breakfast when she had declined their offers to show her the town. And meals had been a waste of time. She picked at her food, too excited to eat, allowing the waiters to take away the courses without sampling more than a mouthful. Now her empty stomach growled in protest, and Moira clapped her hand tight across the offending place. How terrible it would be if her stomach disgraced her in a romantic moment. She would die of embarrassment.

Wondering if Tracey had purchased anything from the snack bar as she sometimes did, Moira walked along the corridor to her friend's room, hoping to beg a snack. So far today she had avoided Tracey, feeling disloyal because of her excitement over her date with the other girl's boy friend.

Long before Moira reached Tracey's room she could hear the radio playing Neapolitan songs, which meant that Tracey was home.

"Come in, door's unlocked," was the reply as Moira tapped on her door.

Tracey was propped against a mountain of bed pillows, balancing a writing pad against her knees. Thinking that her visitor was the maid, she did not look up until Moira blurted: "I'm going to meet the conte this afternoon."

There, it was out. The sentence seemed to explode by itself, without conscious direction. Moira's earth-shattering news was received with such lack of interest that she wondered if Tracey had even heard the announcement.

"He's going to show me around the castello. Do you mind?" she added, feeling obligated to secure Tracey's permission. To her surprise Moira discovered that the other girl was not upset by her news.

"Say, that's great. You'll have the time of your life," Tracey remarked casually, hastily closing a brown folder as Moira stepped toward the bed.

"I'm really looking forward to it," Moira said

with enthusiasm. And she sighed with relief, glad to have her guilty secret in the open, though she was puzzled by Tracey's mild reaction. "If I'm disturbing you, I can come back."

"No, that's okay. Just some work I wanted to finish," Tracey apologized, casually laying a Manila folder on the pink satin bedspread. Grinning at Moira's bright-eyed expectancy Tracey said, "If I know the conte, he'll take you out in his speedboat to complete the tour. He's nuts about the sea. Have you got the right clothes for it?"

"Well, no. I suppose a dress will have to do."

"You've got to be kidding!" Tracey laughed, shaking her head. "Come on, honey, I've got a pair of slacks you can borrow," she offered kindly, crossing to the built-in cupboard beside the hearth. "They're too short for me, so they ought to fit you. They might be a bit of a squeeze around the old excess baggage, but I think you can make it."

She opened the cupboard door to reveal a lavish display of clothing, which turned Moira green with envy. She knew Tracey was only trying to be kind, yet borrowing her elegant clothing would turn the sail into an ordeal.

"Here. These're pretty nautical, don't you think?"

Tracey handed her a pair of white sharkskin slacks, and Moira exclaimed in delight. Down the side seams ran a braid stripe of red and blue anchors, while the wide, flared bell-bottoms were trimmed with the same fabric.

"Oh, I couldn't, really. Thank you anyway."

Ignoring her protest, Tracey held the slacks against Moira's body as she studied the length. "If you wear your white sandals with the two-inch wedge, they'll be okay," she decided, thrusting the slacks into Moira's hands despite her reluctance to accept them. "Think nothing of it."

"You're very kind."

"Easy come, easy go," Tracey quipped, pouring a drink from a pitcher on the tray beside her bed. "Want some juice?"

"Thanks. I really didn't come to borrow clothes," Moira revealed, carefully laying the slacks on the end of the bed.

"What did you want to borrow — apart from my guy, of course?"

Though Moira knew the remark was meant in humor, its implication made her uneasy. "If you don't think I should go —" she began, hesitating beside the bed.

"Don't be silly. I don't own him. You'll find Carlo does exactly as he pleases. If he asked you out today, it's you he wants. Tomorrow it'll probably be someone else." Moira's friend dismissed the topic casually, swinging her long, tanned legs onto the bedspread.

As she listened to the flippant observation, Moira found her happiness ebbing away.

"You're really pretty innocent, you know," Tracey said, turning serious as she studied

Moira's face, which had flushed dusky pink, her sun-darkened freckles showing clearly against her nose.

"It's just that I didn't realize he was like that," she whispered at last. In all her pleasant anticipation of this afternoon she had given little thought to the conte's reputation with other women.

"Well, don't go into a decline over it. Everyone knows that Carlo's a good-time boy. The only thing to do is enjoy the good times when they include you and don't give it a second thought when they don't," Tracey advised sagely.

"Yes," Moira agreed, turning aside, not anxious to have Tracey read anything more in her face. "I suppose that's the sensible way."

She took a couple of breadsticks from Tracey's cluttered lunch tray and wandered to the unshuttered windows. From here Moira could see a small island set in a peaceful mountain lake. It was little more than an overgrown garden of lush vegetation massed in brilliant color around the ruins of a house. This must be the ruin she had seen from the bus window the day she arrived.

"Looking at the haunted island?" Tracey asked, changing stations on the radio.

"Is that what it's supposed to be?" Moira asked in surprise. "It's too pretty."

"Well, that's what the peasants say. Anyway, don't let Carlo take you there, or you'll be glad of the company of a few ghosts. You can bet he knows just how inexperienced you are. It'll be like a lamb amongst the wolves," Tracey warned with a throaty giggle. "Now scat, I've got to finish this paper."

"Thanks for the pants — and these." Moira smiled shyly, gesturing with the breadsticks, though she no longer felt very hungry.

"Sure thing. You can tell me about it when you get back."

Promising she would do so, Moira left Tracey chewing thoughtfully on the end of her pencil as she reopened her paper folder.

In a way Moira was thankful for Tracey's warning about the conte, though it completely shattered the romantic illusions she had built around him. Last night she had not known of his reputation as an international playboy. And though she really hated to admit it, even to herself, her experience with men of that type was zero.

The guided tour was complete, even to the predicted voyage in the conte's speedboat. Moira had been both thrilled and nervous as he cut expertly between the small, bobbing craft in Santa Maria's natural harbor. Everyone knew the conte, and wherever they went he was greeted with affection. Not until the evening shadows grew long and the brilliance of the sky began to dim did she realize how weary she had grown.

During the first moments of the tour, in a

burst of informality, the conte had insisted that she call him Carlo; yet, despite this request, Moira knew he was not wholly at ease with her. Tracey's warning about his fickle nature had made her expect a completely different man. So far Carlo had made no effort to win her with compliments. There had been no staged seduction. The discovery was almost a disappointment. Tracey's revelation had forced Moira to mentally steel herself for a battle that had not taken place.

"Have you enjoyed today?" he asked, driving under the striped awning of the hotel entrance.

"It was wonderful. Thank you," she whispered, her eyes sparkling with pleasure.

"Thank *you*." He smiled as he opened the door of the white sports car, offering his arm in assistance. "Would you like to see the garden at sunset? It's lovely then."

Moira agreed, sighing happily as she caught the envious glances of two girls on the terrace. They were probably wondering why the conte wasted his time on a dumpy nobody with a sunburned nose, and as she had wondered the same thing, Moira could not blame them.

They walked for almost thirty minutes, making polite small talk and enjoying the serene beauty of the park. And while she walked, Moira thought pleasurably about the afternoon.

First he had shown her the vast castello, taking her to the private wing where he and his brother lived. Now Moira understood why she had not seen Sergio since his arrival. Here he remained aloof from the common people, enjoying the privacy of his home in splendid, if slightly reduced, apartments. The rooms were furnished with antiques and the walls were covered by paintings, many of them portraits of Carlo's ancestors. Renaissance scholars rubbed elbows with fierce soldiers, jostling each other for space along staircases and corridors. In the more-elaborate public rooms of the castello were pieces carefully selected to display good taste, while here she saw the more personal mementos of a family who had occupied the same dwelling for centuries. This, and because Carlo was more informal in his own apartments, made Moira prefer them.

In the massive hall where the guests dined, below the carved minstrel's gallery, was a glass showcase where a collection of jewelry was displayed. A special alarm protected the lighted display case from thieves, the tripping device known only to the family and the local police. These, Carlo told her, were the contessa's jewels, hereditary gems passed to the conte's wife through succeeding generations. Though they were magnificent, the gold settings obscured by hundreds of rubies and emeralds that glinted in the light, the heirlooms were not beautiful. There was a massive clumsiness about the pieces, which, to Moira's taste, made them ugly.

She could tell that Carlo was proud of his home as he showed her the good and bad points of living in a castello. To her surprise, when they were out of the public eye he became quietly serious, as though the laughing, sophisticated playboy-conte was only a character he assumed when the occasion demanded.

Now, at the lakeside, he had grown moody, until Moira was afraid to disturb him, so faraway was the expression on his face. Once today he had asked if she were sure they had not met before, and Moira hoped that he had not noticed the flush of guilt she could not hide. That the resemblance was to Elspeth she did not doubt. Did memories of Elspeth occupy his thoughts?

The view was lovely, and she concentrated on the water, watching the lake come alive as sunset turned the rippling water to a brilliant canvas of color. Carlo had told her that the castello had once been surrounded by the lake, which had been used as a moat in the middle ages. Now it was only a picturesque ornament, covering over three acres of the gardens.

"I think the lake is lovely," Moira whispered, watching the water turn silver and red beneath the sun.

"You wouldn't say that if you knew its sinister reputation," he said, coming to life at her words.

"Tracey told me it was haunted. Is that true?"

Carlo shrugged at the question. "Ask me when I've been confronted by an unearthly presence."

"As I said last night, you're very lucky to have

a beautiful home like this. And today I'm completely sober," she added with a shamefaced laugh.

"The castello is a millstone around my neck." Carlo sighed, surprising her by his statement. "Someday the revered old heap of rock will slide into this picturesque lake."

"You're joking, of course!" she cried, as a smile came to his face.

The brilliant sunset gilded Carlo's features, so that he appeared as a statue chiseled from gold. During the boat ride his hair had blown into crisp curls across his brow, giving him a boyish appearance. Now, as she openly admired him in the glow from the water, Moira flushed to realize that she was hoping he would embrace her in this idyllic setting, where they seemed isolated from the world. The fact that they were in full view of hundreds of hotel windows never entered her mind. When she had such treacherous feelings Moira forced herself to remember that Tracey had stood here in this same situation — and, more sadly, Elspeth, too. Perhaps she did not appeal to Carlo, she thought in disappointment, pushing aside her daydreams.

"One of the guests was telling me that this area was damaged during the war," Moira said aloud, forcing her mind to a conversational vein. "You were fortunate that the castello was spared."

"Fortunate!" he snapped, his face tensing with anger. "You know nothing about it."

Shocked by his swift retort, Moira drew back.

"I'm sorry, I . . ."

His face only inches from hers, Carlo spat. "This castello was not harmed during the war — not one building was damaged nor one shrub in the garden. Do you know why?"

Moira shook her head, wondering if she wanted to learn the answer. There was something frightening about his eyes.

"This property was spared through the efforts of my mother, the contessa, preserved intact so her beloved son could inherit his rightful property."

"How did she do that?"

"Do you really want to know? Do you think your gentle British upbringing can stand it?" he demanded sarcastically, and she felt his bruising grip through the fabric of her sleeve.

"I want to know."

"I was only a toddler at the time, but I remember. God, how I remember!" He dropped his hand and stared broodingly at the dark water, his voice low with emotion.

"My father was with the Resistance. We were under German rule then, but being remotely situated, there was little reminder here at the castello. One day the Germans rode up the hill on their motorbikes, their colonel in a sidecar. A fat, dissipated creature, insufferably pompous, he strutted about my home as if he already owned it."

"Where was your father?"

Carlo smiled, but the expression turned bitter.

"They had captured him the week before, but he escaped. My father was clever. But, unfortunately, so were they — and great judges of character. To cut the story short, the German offered my mother her husband in exchange for the castello. She, thinking my father had already been recaptured, revealed his hiding place. Within the hour he was back in prison."

"How terrible," Moira whispered in sympathy, understanding what an effort it was for him to speak about it.

"There's much more," he said, turning toward her, "*much* more. As you probably noticed from her portraits, my mother was very beautiful. The colonel had an eye for beauty, so he offered a new bargain — his original offer with one difference: she was to live here, too . . . with him."

"And she refused?"

"Is that what you would have done?"

"Of course."

Carlo patted her arm as he turned toward the castello, which appeared dark and sinister as the sun disappeared behind the mountains.

"My mother accepted his terms."

A gasp of surprise escaped Moira's lips before she could bite it back, for she had been so sure that the outcome had been otherwise.

"My mother was made of sterner stuff. This she took in stride, a sacrifice at all costs to save the castello. They shot my father that afternoon, then displayed his body in the square. They made me watch. It's a sight I'll not easily forget.

But worse than that is the memory of the next morning, when my mother had breakfast in bed with that fat pig."

The words were spat out with vehemence, and Moira instinctively slipped her hand in his, offering comfort. Though she had expected rejection, Carlo's fingers closed around hers, warmly affectionate.

"I'm sorry. It must have been terrible for you."

"Perhaps you've wondered why my younger brother is a blond," he said after a long silence.

"Well, I suppose I had, now that you mention it," Moira agreed.

"His father's name was Helmut Kauffman."

"The German colonel?"

"Yes. And even harder to bear for a small child, Sergio was the apple of my mother's eye."

"What happened to the colonel?"

Carlo shrugged, drawing away. "Who knows? Smuggled to South America, perhaps." He walked toward the benches at the edge of the garden. "Come on, it's chilly by the water."

His story had brought a lump to Moira's throat. There was such bitterness in his voice, such sadness that she longed to comfort him. Yet when she joined him on the marble bench beneath the trees, Moira saw that he was smiling.

"I don't know why I told you all that," he apologized, taking a cigarette case from his pocket. "Do you smoke?"

"No."

"Good. I prefer a lady not to smoke. In that respect I'm old-fashioned." Carlo lit his cigarette and smoked in silence for a few minutes before continuing. "I wanted you to know what an obligation it is to maintain this place, I suppose. Today you were so impressed that I could not help wondering what you would think if you knew what it had cost the del Santa Marias to keep their castello. Oh, not in terms of money, though it does take the earth to run," he added with a laugh, "but in pride and blood."

"You're right, I hadn't realized," Moira agreed thoughtfully, "but it was done for a purpose. They suffered to keep their memory alive. The castello is Santa Maria's monument. It has survived through the centuries, and even though the walls joining it to the town are gone, people can still look up to the hill and be reminded of the past."

His applause brought a flush of embarrassment to her face, and she wished that she had not been carried away by emotion.

"Well put! I recognize the reader of romantic literature. Ah, come now, I'm only teasing," he apologized, slipping his hand beneath her elbow. "You're the only person I've ever told."

His words made her more confident about their relationship, and Moira looked toward the hotel, where hundreds of lights glittered in the dusk. "Showing others your home is a wonderful gesture."

"By 'show' do you mean turning it into a hotel?"

"Yes. Thousands of people can admire what was once for only an elite few."

"Do you think I like these strangers walking through my home?" Carlo demanded with flashing eyes. "Are you that stupid? I tolerate them because I need their money."

The vehemence of his words left Moira stunned. "I thought you liked it as a hotel," she managed at last, feeling almost as stupid as he had accused her of being.

"Well, if you thought that, you're a fool, too!" Carlo spat, turning away. "It proves you do not know me very well."

Color flushed Moira's cheeks, her temper mounting, until she cried, "You're right. I don't know you well, and I certainly don't intend to!"

Turning on her heel, she fled toward the gardens, dodging marble statues and urns overgrown with vines. At last, breathless and footsore, she sank to a bench, where she began to cry, her nerves taut after the day's events.

He came toward her. How long she had wandered through the dusky garden, Moira did not know. She had thought that Carlo had returned to his precious home long ago. But he came through the long grass, where the dew of evening was already settling in jeweled drops, the expression on his dark face still haughty, but the anger had gone.

"I'm sorry. Can you forgive me for what I said?"

Kneeling before her, he took her hand, and though Moira tried to steel herself against his appeal, she lost the battle.

"I didn't realize —" She sniffled, accepting the handkerchief he proffered to wipe her eyes. "You always seem so happy."

"Only because I'm a good actor," he whispered, lifting her damp hair from her brow. "Please, forget what I said. I was a hot-tempered idiot."

"You're forgiven."

"To prove that's true, will you accept an invitation for tomorrow? You must say 'yes,' because on the weekend we'll be swamped with guests," he pleaded, drawing her against his shoulder. "Seeing that you ferret out my secrets so well, there's one more I want to share. I'll take you to the island. It's best in the morning when the dew is on the flowers."

Starry-eyed, Moira leaned toward him, smelling the warm fragrance of his shaving lotion and wishing that the moment would last forever. "I'd love to come," she breathed.

There was a phone call for Carlo when they returned to the hotel, and with profuse apologies he let Moira go upstairs alone. With mixed emotions she climbed the broad staircase, glancing over her shoulder to see him conversing animatedly, waving his hands and shrugging as he talked. She was in love with him. That dream state in which she had indulged on the beach was only fantasy. Now that she knew the real Carlo, she realized that he was not what she had been warned against by Tracey.

Moira changed out of the borrowed slacks and went to return them. Though the radio was playing as usual, there was no reply when she tapped on Tracey's door. The door was ajar, and she could see that there was no one inside. Tracey must have popped out for a few minutes. Moira laid the slacks on the bed, knowing she would feel better when they were safely returned.

As she turned to go, she saw a Manila folder on the nightstand, the same one in which Tracey had been writing this afternoon. Whoever had put it there had been in such a hurry that several newspaper clippings had fallen to the carpet. Thinking to do Tracey a favor, Moira stooped to pick them up, recoiling at the faded headline: "Famous Model Killed in Accident." With shock she turned over the other clippings to find that they all concerned Elspeth's accident, though two were in Italian and she could understand only the name.

The unexpected surprise of finding these newspaper accounts made Moira feel faint, and she sat on the edge of Tracey's bed, the Manila folder in her hands. As she expected, it was devoted to notes and clippings about Elspeth. For the next few minutes she read dozens of clippings from papers from around the world, finding a disturbing similarity among the reports. Each stated that the police were making investigations and that the attending physician could not be reached for comment.

The discovery was an unpleasant shock. Before returning the clippings, Moira opened an envelope of pictures that was fastened to the back of the folder. The name "Worldwide" was stamped in red letters across the corner of each photo. The pictures must have been taken shortly before Elspeth's death, for they were of *apres-ski* parties around a fireside. She wore ski clothes in all but one of the pictures. That one was of an elegant black gown with a single ornament, and Moira gasped as she recognized the large jeweled cross around Elspeth's neck as the Breen family heirloom. It was not as valuable as the contessa's jewels, but it was treasured for its antiquity. When Elspeth's personal effects had been received by the family, the cross had not been with them. What could have happened to it? Moira puzzled, as she slipped the photos back into the envelope.

Footsteps in the corridor alerted her, and she thrust the folder on top of the nightstand as Tracey strode into the room. An unguarded expression of surprise crossed the other girl's face before she assumed her usual composure. "Say, you shocked me to death. Have fun?"

"Yes, it was a lot of fun," Moira replied stiffly, unable to completely reassume their casual friendship after her discovery. "Thanks for the slacks."

Tracey nodded, watching Moira's face. "What's wrong? Did Carlo give you the rush act?"

"No, he was quite gentlemanly."

Pulling a face at her description, Tracey crossed to the bed, and because Moira was watching for it, she caught the darting glance as Tracey checked the whereabouts of the folder.

"That *is* a surprise — old Lothario himself behaving like a gentleman: you'll have to convince me."

"Maybe he wasn't feeling like . . ."

Tracey chuckled. "Honey, Carlo's always feeling like . . ."

Back in her room Moira lay across the bed thinking about that folder. The chilling discovery had damped even the excitement over her date with Carlo. Why had Tracey collected that information? Was she working for the police? Now Chris Bern's joking words, when he had suggested that Elspeth's fall had been no accident, returned to haunt her. Could there be truth to his suggestion? If so, what part did Tracey play in the mystery?

Chapter 5

By morning Moira's suspicions had almost evaporated. Perhaps Tracey was writing an article about Elspeth's life and had come to the castello for local color. This simple solution was comforting. Even if Tracey were working on a police matter, it need not end their friendship. The solution would be to ask; but to admit that she knew of the file's existence would be to admit that she had been spying in Tracey's room.

Dressed for her outing to the island, Moira arrived in the lobby to find that a message had been left for her at the desk. She tore open the note, scanning the bold, masculine handwriting to read in dismay: "Called away on important business. Will try to be back this afternoon. Carlo."

The hours dragged while she waited for his return, disappointed by this anticlimax to her plans. The guests for the fashion show were arriving this morning, and the expensive clothing worn by the ladies gave Moira something interesting to watch. From the terrace she had a perfect view of these chic women as they alighted from chauffeur-driven cars.

"Hey, do you spend all your time out here?" Chris asked with a laugh.

"I had an engagement, but it was called off," she explained lightly, trying not to let her disappointment show in her voice.

"Was it with the conte?" he asked, surprising Moira by his question.

"As a matter of fact, it was. How did you know?"

"Oh, word gets around. Like to live dangerously, huh?"

"He's really very nice when you get to know him."

"Sure, that's what all the girls think. Well, got to string up a few thousand miles of cable. Coming to the show?"

"I haven't an invitation."

"That's no problem, sweetheart. I'm the one who sets up the place cards." Chris winked. "How do you fancy a spot near the celebrities? We've a few movie stars jetting in tomorrow."

Moira gasped in delight. "I'd love it! Can you get me in?"

"It's already done," he assured, absently stroking her hair. "I'll fix you up with a company dress. Blue ought to do the trick — go great with that hair. By the way, take it easy with the conte — wouldn't want you to be sorry about anything," Chris warned before striding away.

His concern was touching. But it was a pity people kept warning her about Carlo as if she were a babe in arms. Their lectures made her feel schoolgirlishly naive. After all, she had had some boy friends; it was not as if she had been in a convent for twenty-four years. The way Tracey and Chris acted, anyone would think she expected Carlo to be a boy scout. Good heavens! If Tracey had known she was going to the island with him, there would have been a lecture. Friends or no friends, she was not obligated to give them an account of all her movements.

Lunchtime arrived at last. Meeting her in the doorway of the dining hall, Tracey accompanied Moira to the table. They looked with interest at the sets that had been erected for the weekend fashion show. The theme of the collection was the Renaissance, and this castello was the perfect place to preview Sergio's winter show.

Though Tracey had not seen the collection, she told Moira that it featured velvets and silk damasks trimmed in fur and jewels. The scoop had been revealed by Sergio himself over cocktails on the terrace. The designs had been inspired by paintings in Italian galleries, and the fashion world eagerly awaited what the press was calling "Campella's Botticelli period." The hall would be transformed to a medieval banqueting hall, complete with silken banners and costumed minstrels.

Throughout the first course, workmen hammered the finishing touches to a raised dais at the end of the hall, over which was draped a scarlet velvet curtain edged in gold with the del Santa Maria coat of arms embroidered in the center.

A disturbance at the entrance took Moira's

attention as she was finishing her dessert. By the stiff, bowing politeness of the previously relaxed waiters Moira knew that the conte had returned. She was not, however, prepared for the shock that followed, transforming her smile of welcome to a frown of dismay. Carlo was accompanied by a girl, an elegant female who prowled rather than walked, her swishing red palazzo pants giving fluidity to her steps.

"Did you get my message, signorina?" Carlo asked Moira as they walked by.

All she could do was nod, so taken aback was she by his companion. Was she the business that had called him away? Moira wondered in silent misery.

"Chalk up another one." Tracey grinned. "Wonder where he picked her up." And she turned in her seat to take in the details of the new arrival's clothes. "Bet that's a Campella."

Moira nodded, thankful that Tracey did not know how crushed she felt. It would have been too humiliating to have told her about their date and then have Carlo come in with another girl. Tracey would think she was naive to have fallen for that line.

Moira walked disconsolately toward the door. Well, it's been a good lesson, she reminded herself bravely, squaring her shoulders. We live and learn, as Tracey is fond of saying.

"Don't run away from me."

The words made Moira stiffen, her emotions battling for control. Of all the nerve! Now Carlo is going to act as if nothing is wrong, she thought in indignation.

He caught her arm, drawing her against an arrangement of ferns and lilies overflowing the huge urns at the dining-hall entrance. Pride told Moira to haughtily break free of his demanding grasp and tell him what she thought of his "important business," but her wavering heart would not allow it.

"You're angry."

"Shouldn't I be?"

"No. My business was real; the lady, just an old friend," Carlo explained, his eyes smiling.

The fascination he held for her was too much; anger dissipated before the warmth of his manner, and she whispered, "I'm so glad that's all."

Because she wanted to believe him, Moira did not notice the triumph that flickered in his smile. And when he offered his arm, she willingly clung to the soft fabric of his jacket.

"It is too hot now for the island," he stated, leading her to the terrace. "Have you been to the beach yet?"

"Yes, but I was disappointed in it."

"If you were disappointed, it's because you didn't find the right place. Leave it to me. I know the perfect spot. Though the Adriatic is too warm for swimming, we can lie on the sand," he suggested, his face lighting with enthusiasm. "Get your suit and meet me in the lobby."

"What was your important business, anyway?"

Moira asked later as they pulled up beneath two tall umbrella pines, standing sentinel beside the twisting coastal highway.

"Nothing important." He dismissed it, reaching into the backseat for her beach bag. "Family interests — very boring. I'd sooner have been with you."

At his compliment Moira smiled happily, surveying the wide expanse of golden beach, where a handful of striped umbrellas dotted the sand.

Carlo opened the trunk of the car and took out a folding beach umbrella and a picnic cooler. While he set up the umbrella, Moira raced back to the car for her suntan lotion, which must have fallen from her bag when he had pulled it over the seat. The plastic tube was on the floor among some newspapers. To her surprise she saw today's date on a German-language paper printed in Berne. Had Carlo been to Switzerland? Surely he could not have driven there and back for lunch. But though she glanced about the car, Moira saw no evidence of luggage labels or airline-ticket envelopes.

Could he have gone to fetch that girl? she thought uncomfortably, as they lay on the warm sand. Was that why he had made the sudden journey? One glimpse of the devastating creature in red had given Moira an inferiority complex.

"Where did you go this morning?" she asked, trying to sound casual, but inside her stomach flopped with the fear that her suspicions were accurate.

"You're very inquisitive. If you must know, I went to Ravenna. It's several hours' journey, so I had to get up very early — too soon to wake you," he explained, flashing his charming smile, which had the power to melt her toes to jelly.

Moira smiled back, though she wished he had said instead, "I flew to Switzerland." After all, his having a foreign newspaper in his car was a poor reason to suspect Carlo of lying. He could have purchased the Swiss paper in Ravenna.

"Do you read German?" she asked after a pause, letting the hot yellow sand trickle through her fingers.

Carlo frowned at her question. "I came here to relax. Now I demand a moratorium on questions. Close your eyes and sunbathe!"

Laughing, she obeyed his command, though Moira could not help wondering why he had chosen not to reply to her question.

The roll of the sea and the screeching of birds in the distance blended pleasantly with the strains of lively music carrying from a roadside trattoria. Gradually Moira relaxed. The combination of Chris's warnings and Tracey's folder on Elspeth had made her suspect everyone of dark, sinister deceptions. It was really silly when she was on the beach with the most handsome man she had ever seen. And a conte at that. Handsome, rich, and so flatteringly attentive — what more could she ask?

"For once I think you're relaxed," he whispered, as she burrowed her toes in the hot sand. "Where's that stiff upper lip?"

"Why do you always tease me?" Moira demanded, half in anger, stopping when she saw his delighted smile at her emotion, that fascinating expression that revealed those incredibly white teeth.

Carlo shrugged. "Who knows?" He was staring at the sea. "Maybe I tease because I'm unsure of how to behave with you. You're different from the others who come here."

Moira snorted in annoyance. "I'm not as different as you seem to think," she cried. "I'm not as pretty as they are, or as fashionable, but inside I'm not different."

Carlo regarded her intently, moving closer over the abrasive heat of the sand. Beneath the striped gaudiness of the huge umbrella they had complete privacy.

"I wonder . . ." he began slowly, reaching for her hand.

Moira's heart pounded as he squeezed her fingers. Bending over her, his face dark, Carlo brushed her cheek with his lips.

"Yes, I suppose you are like the others in some respects. But you are a romantic . . . and I haven't the heart —" he decided as he abruptly pulled away.

In disappointment Moira stared at him, puzzled and hurt by his withdrawal. "Haven't the heart for *what?*" she insisted.

"You don't really know me, only the part you wish to know."

"If you think I'm afraid of being kissed —" she began, propping herself on one elbow and banging her head against the heated fabric of the umbrella.

But he only smiled at her anger. Lazily he pushed her back. "Not afraid, perhaps, but not prepared."

Moira shivered at the expression on his face, and when Carlo bent to kiss her, the heat of his mouth was a shock.

Tracing his hand over the white skin of her shoulder, he asked, "Why have you no freckles here?"

Lulled by happiness, Moira closed her eyes, finding his caressing hand pleasantly stirring. "Because I usually have my shoulders covered. Ireland is a lot cooler than Santa Maria."

"And this, too," he murmured after a moment.

Coming back to earth, Moira gasped with shock, for he had slid the strap of her bathing suit from her shoulder. Mesmerized, she stared at the contrast of his brown fingers as he stroked her white skin, as he pushed the strap lower. Suddenly Moira came alive. With a squeal she pushed him away, clutching the falling strap in shocked modesty, trying to slip it back, but the suntan oil had made her skin slippery.

"How dare you?" she demanded, thrusting him away, pushing her toes against his slick satin bathing trunks.

Carlo smiled at her anger. "See?" he said with

a grin, "You *are* different from the others. You're a modest virgin."

With this he scrambled to his feet and sprinted over the sand, plunging into the warm sea.

Trembling with emotion, Moira collected her belongings, thrusting them into the beach bag. The boldness of his action made her tremble, but her anger was directed as much at herself as at Carlo, for she had enjoyed his touch.

"Hey, don't go!" Carlo shouted, seeing her trekking up the sandy incline toward the parked car. "Wait."

In a few minutes he had joined her, slipping his white slacks over his still-wet bathing suit. Conscious of her trembling lip, Moira turned away, stiffening at the heat of his hand on her back.

"I only wanted to show you that you're different," he explained. "Admit it."

Silently Moira watched him button his striped shirt, which he had draped like a brilliant sail from the antenna of the sports car. Aware of her own near-nakedness, she drew her striped beach robe over her head, defiantly pulling up the zipper.

"Now that your modesty's assured in that Bedouin tent, will you speak to me?"

"I don't know why I should. You brought me here deliberately —" Moira began, her voice barely under control.

"Of course I did." Carlo dragged open the car door. When she refused to get inside, he shrugged and went to the trunk to return the umbrella. "We agreed, remember?" he called from the depths of the trunk, as he struggled with the telescoping aluminum pole.

"To come for sunbathing, that's all."

"That's all that happened. Come on, get in — or are you intending to walk back?"

The challenge was one she would have loved to accept, but the sun was hot and Moira was not sure of the way. With dignity she slipped inside the car, her terrycloth robe clinging damply to the upholstery. In such a small space it was difficult to sit very far from him, but she squeezed against the door until the armrest cut bruisingly into her hipbone.

They drove in silence, whipping around curves, until Moira found her heart in her mouth. She glanced at his set face, tension apparent in his lean jaw. Though Carlo seemed angry, there was an expression of near pleasure as he took the curves with expertise, as if he enjoyed the challenge. At last she was forced to speak out of self-preservation.

"Please slow down. You're right — I'm not like the others." Her words, forming an apology as they did, were hard to voice.

He grinned, and immediately let up the accelerator. "All right, I accept your apology."

Bristling under his smug assurance, Moira wanted to shout, "It's not an apology! It's because I don't want to end up at the foot of the cliff." But she let him have his moment of triumph. About one fact he was right: she did not know him. Every meeting seemed to bring forth a different person. Had he play-acted so long that he did not even know himself?

By the time they approached the town, Carlo had come as close to an apology as he intended. His hand rested warmly on hers, and Moira was almost glad that they had quarreled, for after the emotion of her outburst she felt spent and happy.

"Have you explored the town yet?" he asked.

"Yes, between dodging Miss Cross and Mrs. Kay."

Carlo slowed the car to a crawl in the cobbled streets where the tall houses almost scraped the sides of the vehicle. Laughing children waved to them from doorsteps as they passed, and he tooted the horn in greeting.

Siesta must be over, for shutters were coming down and local shopkeepers began putting their most tempting merchandise on display: hand-made galleons and knitted goods, silk from the mills at Como, Venetian glass goblets and Austrian embroidered blouses, fish and lilies, long loaves of bread, and strings of pungent cheeses. Every shop offered temptations for the tourists, who could be seen ambling from under the striped awnings of cafes or sipping drinks in the shade of the flowering oleanders.

"Though we need their money, tourists have made these people cannibals," Carlo observed sadly. "Once they were content to fish and pick olives. Now look at them, greedily rubbing their hands and counting change. It's very sad."

"They have more luxuries now."

"True. Some of them even have cars, whereas once they hauled produce on sleds up the alleys. In that respect it's better, but at the same time worse. They're not amusing children, as they once were. They grow paunchy and middle-aged, softened by the easy living. Their greed has become a sickness."

"Is that why you resent making the castello a hotel?"

"That's one reason. They are simple people, and education is not stressed as it should be. Feudally they look toward their conte for instruction. What can I say to them when I operate a hotel, when I allow the home of my ancestors to become a lodging house?"

"If you hadn't done that, we'd never have met," Moira ventured shyly, lifting the expression of gloom that had descended over his face.

"I love little girls who cheer me up," he confided with a smile as they left the town, laboring up the road toward the castello. "It's cooler now. Would you like to go to the island after all — if I promise to behave?"

He was laughing at her, yet his humor was not unkind.

"May I change? I'd feel more comfortable."

"Of course, though you might be better off in a swimsuit. Beaching the boat can sometimes be tricky."

Racing to her room, Moira dressed in the clothes she had worn that morning. Her hair was too flyaway to be arranged, so she left it loose. On an inspiration she snapped a creamy camellia from a flower arrangement on the landing to pin in her hair.

Soon Moira was scrambling over slippery rocks on the shoreline, water oozing through her tennis shoes. Behind her Carlo beached the boat, wading through the shallows, where trailing moss clung to the soaked bottoms of his canvas slacks.

The island was a secret hideaway. Though almost within shouting distance of the bustling hotel, it seemed like another world. Through the screen of trees the somber, battlemented castello was visible. The shield of green merged with blue sky, the brilliant colors making it like a giant postcard in the distance. At the water's edge knotted cypresses projected from the lake, gnarled branches twisted in grotesquely human postures. Moira turned her back on the sinister trees rising like an army of tormented beings from the depths of the lake.

"They are ugly," Carlo remarked with a grin. "When I was a boy my nurse frightened me with tales of wicked children turned to trees by the witch of the lake. She was so convincing a story-teller that for years I was afraid to beach the boat on this side of the lake."

"Oh, there's another landing?" Moira asked in surprise, glancing about the tangled shrubbery for a jetty, but she saw none.

"It's on the other side of the villa. There's a road to the highway."

His hand on her arm, Carlo guided Moira up the shingled beach, their feet crunching on the shifting ground where foliage from the gardens encroached in tangled green streamers.

"These gardens must have been lovely once," Moira exclaimed breathlessly, clutching the warm strength of Carlo's hand as they reached a half-buried path to the villa.

"This was the conte's plaything, a . . ." He paused, his brow wrinkling as he sought the English word.

"A folly. That's what they call those things in Britain."

"That's right. He had plants from all over the world in these gardens. They say it was such a showplace that royalty came here to play at being peasants."

"Why did they let it fall into ruin?"

He shrugged eloquently. "Perhaps following generations didn't value such an expensive plaything. Come, I'll show you the villa."

Abruptly he turned, as if afraid to say more, and he broke their handclasp. Moira followed him, disappointed that the contact was ended, for seeing his bronzed fingers twined in her own had caused a chill of pleasure to creep along her spine.

Terraced pathways wound about the weathered stone ruin. Parts of the villa were in good repair, while others were a total shell, the red-tiled roof gaping open to the sky. The three-storied villa was of warm yellow stone, crumbled and sun-bleached like many of the buildings in Santa Maria. The walls were covered by flowering vines, which crept with tenacious fingers beneath the huge slabs of rock, undermining the foundations in places with broad, beelike branches. Wisteria cascading in long ribbons met lilacs and japonicas in varied hues from red to blue. Missing from the landscape were the pots of geraniums that cluttered doorsteps and windows in the town. This villa was too wild for anything as neatly cultivated as a pot of geraniums, and the untamed splendor of the scene made Moira shiver with a mixture of emotions she did not understand.

Watching her, Carlo smiled, his face softening. "I'm glad you find her beautiful, too."

"Her?" Moira questioned.

"Yes. Such a lovely place could never be a 'he.' The villa is like a woman — beautiful, tempestuous."

"That describes some women, but not me," she confessed candidly, waiting for a reaction; but instead he laughed, and stepping through the bushes, beckoned her to follow.

They were inside a courtyard, the floor overgrown with foliage and weeds. A mosaic of blue and white was still visible beneath the greenery, and Moira gasped at the unexpected beauty of its design. The walls arched into a dozen doorways leading to the still darkness of the ruin.

"Come on, are you afraid?" He laughed, seeing her hesitance as she paused in the courtyard, summoning courage to venture through those shadowed arches.

"Not with you," Moira decided, stepping toward him. "But you must admit, it looks like a Roman ruin. I half expect someone in a toga to appear from inside."

Carlo laughed in delight at her description. "What an imagination you have! I assure you, this is definitely not old enough to harbor Roman ghosts. The only ghost, besides the witch of the lake, of course, is a poor lady who drowned herself several centuries ago."

He paused, and Moira was surprised by the strange expression that came to his face, robbing it of humor, turning the dark eyes strangely frightening. Though she wanted to say something amusing, Moira was unable to think of any quips, such as Tracey would have used, so she waited silently for him to speak. Carlo shook off his sudden black mood and turned to her with a flashing smile.

"The legend says that this lady compels others to drown themselves. Do you believe in legends?"

"In a place like this it would be easy to believe anything."

"That's right. When there's a storm you imagine you can hear cries in the wind."

She shuddered, and Carlo laughingly caught her arm, drawing her against him. The gesture was so unexpected that Moira dropped her crocheted bag, spilling the contents on the floor. But she did not notice, for Carlo's arms were about her, and his mouth, strong and sweet, came down on hers.

When he drew away, his face was serious. "I am sorry," he said simply, his hands opening in empty gesture. "Here, let me help you pick up your things."

It was then that Moira realized that her purse was on the ground. Carlo had already gathered her lipstick and comb from a bed of flowering vine. In dismay Moira saw that her wallet had fallen open, and there, staring up at her, was the picture of Elspeth that she always carried. Grabbing for the wallet, hoping to keep her guilty secret, Moira only touched the corner before Carlo had it in his grasp. Together they stood, and he almost closed the wallet with the picture inside. She was nearly safe, but something made him look down, and when he did, Moira saw shock and disbelief on his face.

"To the only sister I ever knew. Love, Elspeth," he read, while Moira stood dumbfounded, her mind a blank.

If she had prepared an explanation, perhaps things could have been smoothed over. If she could even think — but all she could concentrate on was the expression on his face. Angry disillusionment turned him haughty, until she was coldly shut out. With anguish Moira remembered the warmth of his kiss. Things had been so right today. Above all the girls here, he had chosen her to accompany him to his island. Now it was ruined, because she had not had the courage to disclose her relationship to Elspeth in the beginning.

"I see you knew my fiancee," he remarked sarcastically, handing back the closed wallet. "You must forgive me for being surprised. I didn't know that Elspeth had a sister."

"She wasn't my sister. We were cousins," Moira explained tearfully. "I should have told you, but I didn't want you to be hurt."

His expression cut short further explanation. With a spin of his heel Carlo was already on the first level of the terrace. "I just remembered some work I must attend to," he said tersely, refusing to turn round.

"Why won't you let me explain?" Moira pleaded as she started after him, close to tears. "It's because I didn't want to stir unpleasant memories. Between us it didn't seem important."

"You're right. It's not important. After all, we are barely removed from strangers."

They reached the shore, where he silently helped her aboard the boat, untying the mooring and pushing it into the water. On the short return journey Moira sat in misery, desperately searching for an explanation for withholding her relationship to Elspeth. It was useless. By his expression she knew he had shut her out. There was only emptiness in his face.

Chapter 6

Two hours had not erased the anguish and embarrassment of the confrontation at the villa. Had Moira not cared for Carlo, the scene would have been distressing enough, but adoring him as she did made it doubly painful. The stony silence in which they had returned to the hotel had been broken once, when, brown eyes flashing with anger, he had turned fiercely upon her to shout: "I don't like being tricked. Once I loved your cousin, but she used me. I never want to hear her name again!"

Reviewing his statement now, in a more detached state, Moira realized that had been wrenched from him in anger. If Sergio had spoken of betrayal, she could have understood — but not Carlo, the man for whom Elspeth had left her first love. To recall the anger blazing in Carlo's face made her shudder. He had been like a stranger. It had been a mistake not to have told him who she was, but certainly the omission did not merit such bitter anger. The hurt was doubly painful when she recalled how dreamily she had wondered if he, too, were falling in love.

Moira stayed in the alcove from where she had watched the others dine. Though only two people were aware of the quarrel, she did not mingle with the guests in case, in a fit of temper, Carlo should reveal her identity. Had she reasoned with herself, Moira would have realized that such an outburst was unlikely, for Carlo was his most charming at the evening meal. The guests expected the privilege of dining with the conte, like being seated at the captain's table aboard ship. Despite this reassuring fact Moira had not the confidence to act as if nothing were wrong, although she had left the safety of her room. Why shut herself away? The conte was not the only man in the world.

"Who'm I trying to convince?" she muttered aloud, glaring at a painting across the hall, the light catching only the face of a goddess surrounded by a group of cherubs. Politely the canvas deity stared back, her painted face blank, beautiful eyes and bow-shaped lips reminding Moira of her own plainness.

"Oh, what do you know!" she grumbled in exasperation.

"Excuse, please." A woman's voice jerked Moira back to sanity. What a crackpot she must appear, talking to a painting!

"I'm sorry, am I in your way?" she mumbled, moving her feet from the narrow walkway. Glancing up in confusion, Moira saw a familiar face but could not place the woman in pink who smiled politely at her as she swished past.

The flickering wall sconce flashed fire from the woman's necklace, and Moira gasped with sudden shock, her gaze riveted on the dazzling pool. That silver cross set with yellow-brown gems was unmistakable: it was Elspeth's necklace.

"Excuse me, did you drop your magazine?" Moira called, snatching a magazine from the chest behind her in a desperate bid for a closer look at the jewelry.

"Mine? No, I still have mine," the woman replied, perfect teeth revealed in a polite but puzzled smile.

"How silly of me. It must belong to someone else," Moira apologized lamely. The woman nodded, continuing her journey down the corridor, her carriage regally graceful.

The incident had given Moira only a brief look at the Celtic cross, but it was all the time she needed. The top stone, though polished to a dull plane, had been chipped in the identical place as the Breen family cross. Now she knew why the cross had never arrived at Castle Brennan. By carelessness that woman had implicated herself in the deepening mystery surrounding Elspeth's death.

Moira's first inclination was to bluntly ask the woman where she had gotten it. There was no mistake; that cross had belonged to Elspeth. It was as much Elspeth Breen as her auburn hair or the red carnation that had become a trademark on her suits and gowns.

"Say, hold up."

With a cry of dismay, she collided with Chris, who miraculously saved the partially filled glass he was carrying.

"I'm sorry — my mind was at sea," she apologized, hoping that she sounded convincing and that Chris had drunk enough of whatever was in his glass not to notice her flaming nose and puffy eyes.

"Are you blinded by *Il Conte,* or just myopic?" he joked, steering her safely downstairs. "Guess if you're coming down, I don't want to go to my room after all."

His companionship gave Moira a surge of warmth, welcome after the iciness of Carlo's departure. "You're nice," she whispered impulsively, suddenly wanting to hug him for making her feel better.

"Now I *know* I'll stay," he assured her, catching the fabric of her blouse to draw her closer. "How about a drink?"

"All right, but could we stop a minute?"

"Sure, what's on your mind?"

"Chris, I've got to talk to you."

"Okay, talk." He laughed, guiding her to a corner where two brocade chairs were discreetly shielded by a polished suit of armor. "Now, what is it?"

"Who's that woman?" Moira looked toward the statuesque beauty, who was now laughing quietly with the conte beside the empty fireplace, where both of them appeared at home beneath the massive heraldic emblems and fan-shaped display of ancient swords and halberds.

"You mean the one in pink?"

"Yes."

"Don't tell me you don't recognize her!" Chris laughed in surprise. "I thought you women kept up with the latest fashions. I'll introduce you if you'd like."

"You know her?" Moira gasped.

"Sure. That's Bettina Corri, Sergio's top model — the one who replaced Elspeth Breen. She's a lot like Elspeth really, except for the hair. I guess he digs that type of face."

At Chris's casual remark, Moira found herself studying Bettina Corri in a new light. His observations were correct. When you ignored the different hair color, Bettina Corri's facial structure was identical to Elspeth's, her tall, lithe body and proud carriage heightening the illusion.

With a quick admonition to stay put, Chris set down his glass and headed for the handsome couple beside the mantel. Moira realized that he was going to bring the model to meet her. Could she keep her composure?

When Chris approached with Bettina Corri on his arm, Moira was amazed to see that the cross was gone. A few minutes ago she had seen it with her own eyes, glinting on the woman's pink caftan. Surely she had not imagined it. Yet it appeared so, for the expanse of fuchsia satin was starkly bare. The only jewelry Bettina wore were two jeweled hoops swinging from her ears.

"Here's someone who's crazy to meet you," Chris began, extending his hand toward Moira, who rose woodenly from her chair.

"Moira Connor, meet Bettina."

"Ah, but we have already met. A few minutes ago I fell over you, do you remember?"

Forcing a smile, Moira agreed, fascinated by the beautiful empty face before her. Bettina's high cheekbones were emphasized by her large, darkly outlined eyes, while her towering hairstyle made her neck seem fragilely slender in contrast. In this brilliant light Moira understood why she had thought the woman familiar. It was not just her resemblance to Elspeth, but the fact that Bettina was the one who had accompanied Carlo to lunch today.

A lump rose to her throat, pounding like a drum to choke her words when Moira found that she was looking straight into Carlo's eyes, for he had come to stand beside Bettina.

"Good evening, signorina. I hope you are enjoying your stay with us," he said politely, giving no indication that anything of a more intimate nature had occurred between them.

His distant, impersonal air left Moira speechless. She gasped and cleared her throat, but by then he had whisked Bettina to a circle of laughing acquaintances, leaving Moira stunned and weak.

"Hey, what happened to the big romance?" Chris asked.

"That wasn't anything." Moira dismissed it, turning her back on the couple beside the hearth, unable to bear the sight of Carlo's slender hands resting possessively on Bettina's back. "Just an afternoon date," she mumbled.

Chris sighed with relief. "Gee, I'm glad to hear that." He touched her face, his fingers caressingly warm, then he grinned as he admitted, "It gives me a clear field. This morning I thought the conte had you tied up and labeled. Come on, let's dance."

"I'd rather not," Moira began, but her protests were lost in the surge of violin music as the hotel orchestra began a spirited rendition of a Strauss waltz.

"Forget it. I'm not taking 'no' for an answer," Chris shouted above the music, catching her arm and marching her to the adjoining ballroom.

Not till after midnight did Moira have an opportunity to gather her thoughts. The onslaught of music and laughter, generously laced with champagne, played havoc with her reasoning power. Elspeth's cross floated before her as she danced, and Moira wished that she could handle it to be certain it was not a duplicate. That broken stone was the deciding factor. No one would have reproduced a flaw like that. If there were more to the skiing accident, as the police had suspected at the time, perhaps Bettina Corri was also involved. Though the cross was old, it was certainly not grounds for murder; becoming the top Campella model might be. Surely Bettina would not engineer the murder of a rival . . . and why would Sergio dispose of his top-ranking model? Was jealousy over a broken romance enough to drive him to murder?

The more Moira thought about the situation, the more puzzled she became. To ask either Carlo or Sergio about the accident would be useless. The local police could supply the answers, but then she would be involving officials who might not take kindly to her interference. Why not talk to the doctor who had attended Elspeth? He could surely tell her if there had been anything suspicious about the circumstances of her fall. Getting to the ski country would be the problem. This afternoon, before that terrible scene, Carlo had offered her the use of one of his cars to visit the surrounding countryside. The offer was probably not valid any more, but there was no harm in asking, Moira thought, all those glasses of champagne making her bold. She would ask him tomorrow.

The setting for the Campella Renaissance collection was stunning. Flaring torches and heraldic banners on the castle walls made the past come vividly alive. Even the hotel staff wore medieval livery of crimson and white. A silver embroidered helmeted knight, the conte's heraldic crest, was emblazoned on the chests of the men's shimmering paltocks. The women wore peasant dresses with white bodices and brilliantly striped skirts, the costume completed by laced black velvet stomachers.

The arrangements were breathtaking. Even

before the actual fashion show began, Moira was more than satisfied by the lavish detail. A trestle table was set on the dais at the far end of the banqueting hall. This was where the conte and his important guests would sit. Smaller tables were ranged close to the walls, beneath the stained-glass windows, for the other spectators. Moira had a place reserved for her near the dais. For this stroke of luck she had to thank Chris, who had switched the name cards this morning while the hall was deserted. At such close quarters the celebrities would be clearly visible.

At last it was time to dress for the luncheon. Moira squeezed inside the cornflower-blue velvet gown that Chris had sent to her room. When she saw her reflection she started in surprise at the stranger in the beveled glass. The flowing lines slimmed and lengthened her body, and from this distance not one freckle was visible. As Chris had suggested, she plaited her hair, winding it to form a base for the accompanying coronet, which she secured with hairpins, holding her head erect to prevent the headdress from toppling sideways.

Except for a handful of cameramen and assistants, the banqueting hall was empty. Flickering light from the sconces on the walls cast giant shadows, making sinister movements against the tapestry hangings. When the show began only the battery of camera lights would be on, giving the gloomy hall the appearance of dusk.

The dining tables looked like a film set of the middle ages, with silver bowls of fruit and goblets of wine. Moira made a mental note to eat sparingly, for she suspected that this banquet would consist of many courses. And though it had been customary in the middle ages to dispose of the first courses by vomiting, she was not anxious to become so authentic.

Tonight there would be a dance, to which she had not been invited, but being part of the excitement this afternoon was more than she had expected. If only she had not quarreled with Carlo, this would have completed her too-good-to-be-true vacation. Well, that's what it has been, too good to be true, she thought sadly, fingering the place card bearing her name printed in bold letters. She would have to pretend that things were normal and return Carlo's icy politeness in good measure.

"Ah, what a lovely partner they've given me."

Moira glanced up at an enormous girth of gray-suited flesh, her eyes traveling upward until she encountered a pair of pale eyes buried beneath layers of rosy fat. The man beamed down at her, lumbering between the tables like a giant bear.

"Hello," she greeted him coolly, though she was pleased by the admiration in his face.

"Moira Connor," the stranger read, squinting over her shoulder at her place card. "Ha! A lady buyer from Britain," he declared triumphantly, and without waiting for a reply he rolled toward the nearest cameraman and began a conversation.

As she watched him Moira wondered what a man like that was doing at a fashion show. He must be with one of the ladies who had arrived yesterday. His accent was not Italian, though with his gravelly, rumbling voice it was hard to place. Mr. Bear, she thought with a smile, that's what I'll call him.

Turning her attention to the arriving guests, Moira spent the next half hour in raptures at the dazzling array of nobles who passed before her. Surely the period costumes of this audience would surpass even Sergio's creations. Not everyone was in costume, and the sprinkling of modern dress was glaringly out of place amongst this magnificent cavalcade of history. Though her own dress was an accurate reproduction of a glowing, high-waisted Renaissance gown, the other guests wore an assortment of modes, ranging from Robin Hood jerkins to elaborate padded doubles that would have done justice to the court of Henry the Eighth. On the dais of honor, Carlo, in black trimmed with silver, conversed with a French film star and a haughty Italian princess. Both women were attired in sumptuous creations, slashed and padded, sparkling with brilliants and completed by towering cone-shaped headdresses of brocade, which fluttered trailing draperies when they moved. At close quarters, Moira discovered with surprise, neither of the celebrities did justice to their photographs.

Carlo met her stare, his eyes as coldly appraising as a stranger's, and she quickly turned away, not anxious to have him think she craved his attention.

When the hall was almost filled, Moira's admirer squeezed into place beside her, overflowing from the small dining chair. Winking in recognition, he leaned close to hiss in a wine-laden breath, "I'm in sales, too. Argentina — big, exclusive account."

Wishing he would be quiet, Moira glanced pointedly toward the speaker's rostrum, a draped, castellated balcony at the end of the hall, where Sergio was about to speak. The wooden set looked real from this distance, obscuring the windows and the contessa's jewelry display case behind yards of crimson curtains. The models would enter there, then walk the length of the hall on a red carpet spread over the tiled floor. Chris was right: this was the perfect seat from which to see everything.

"Forgot your note pad. Here," Mr. Bear hissed, thrusting a folded paper and a pencil into Moira's hand, "use this."

Nodding her thanks, Moira accepted his offer, feeling that there was little point in explaining that she was merely a guest. She settled back to enjoy the luncheon as Sergio, resplendent in rose-pink velvet, introduced himself, signaling the start of the banquet.

Long before Mr. Bear had finished eating,

Moira was stuffed. He insisted on passing each dish to her, making sure she took a portion before he would replace the food. It was quite a relief when the spicy dishes were carried from the table.

A cavorting jester in red and yellow parti-colored hose suddenly leaped from the castellated balcony and somersaulted the length of the hall. A round of applause followed his exhibition. Then heralds sounded a rousing fanfare to announce Sergio's appearance.

Moira had never seen such lovely clothes. The only flaw in her enjoyment of the entertainment was the commentary in Italian. She could not understand a word, a situation the attentive Mr. Bear sought to correct with winey translations in a stage whisper, until Moira went pink with embarrassment. On top of this she became aware of Carlo's gaze, fixed intently on her corner of the table as he seemed to pay scant attention to the models. Of course, it could be just his annoyance at Mr. Bear's interruptions, but Moira was enough in love to want it to be otherwise.

The loveliest dress of the collection was modeled by Bettina, who swept the length of the hall amid delighted applause. Her ball gown was of flowing burgundy velvet lavishly trimmed in bright jeweled bands, which edged the bodice and tightly circled the wide sleeves to form three puffs of fabric. Over this she wore a high-collared cloak of silver lame lined in burgundy.

The outfit was completed by a hat of rolled, padded velvet banded with strips of silver, encircling her small head like a halo. Around the room sketch pads and notebooks flashed into view, and Bettina walked slowly, making an extra pass before whisking the creation out of sight. The overhead lighting, which lit only the runway for the models, left the remainder of the room in near darkness. Though effective, the murky colored light filtering from the stained-glass windows made visibility poor for all but the fortunate few on the inner row, hampering the notetakers, who fumed at the inconvenience.

Next season mass-produced versions, trimmed down for the average pocketbook, would make appearances from New York to Dublin.

Sergio's daytime wear, in contrast to the evening clothes, borrowed its inspiration from men's costumes. Long tunics over colored tights and short, hip-touching capes worn with feather-trimmed hats were his designs for winter street wear.

Too chilly for Castle Brennan, Moira thought apprehensively, recalling the sweeping wind that sought every inch of exposed skin. She was aware of Mr. Bear's harsh breathing as he wrote, eyes glued to the models' shapely legs as they paraded before him. It was a relief to have his attention so absorbed; this way he was far too busy to offer any translations.

When the lights came on, Moira slipped into

the crowd to avoid him, though she was not quick enough to escape without notice. He waved his note pad to attract her attention, but she felt justified in ignoring him, thankful to have escaped his clutches.

At the end of the hall Moira looked for Chris to thank him for the excellent seat he had provided for her. She found him perched on a rickety ladder behind the fake battlements, repairing a tear in the backdrop.

"Oh, sure, glad you enjoyed it. You can give me the dress tomorrow."

Another man called to him, and with a grin, Chris jumped to the platform, leaving her alone amidst the cardboard scenery.

Chapter 7

"Sorry I ran off yesterday — didn't mean to desert you," Chris explained over morning coffee, as he took a break from repacking materials not being used in the Sunday showing.

"That's all right. I understand."

"Going to stay on the terrace all day?" he asked with a grin, drawing intricate loops across the top of the menu.

"I really wanted to do some sight-seeing, but I've no car."

"Sorry, can't help you there. Why don't you ask Tracey to lend you hers? She's going sailing, so she won't need it."

"With the conte?" Moira blurted, too fast for thought.

Chris grinned at her embarrassed flush when she realized what she had said. "I thought your big romance was over."

"It is."

"Well, I'll set your mind at ease, sweetheart. Old Trace has latched onto Sergio now. Guess Bettina Corri's too much competition. They'll probably make it a foursome."

Moira digested his words in silence, picturing those three glamorous people lounging aboard Carlo's boat while he skillfully maneuvered the craft to impress the ladies.

When Chris had gone, Moira glowered at the cloudless azure sky, resenting her mental image of that laughing group. Tracey's car! she muttered to herself. It was Carlo's car. He would think she had some nerve expecting to use his property after their quarrel. Still, it was the only way to visit Elspeth's doctor. Already his name and the town where he lived were ingrained in her memory, the discovery made from those revealing newspaper clippings.

Moira came indoors to find Tracey talking to Carlo in the lobby. At the sight of them her first reaction was to call off her plans. But instead of retreating she summoned her courage and walked toward them.

"Good morning," she sang, wearing her most charming smile, conscious that her voice was too loud, her greeting falsely gay.

Both Tracey and Carlo turned in surprise, she to smile in recognition, while his reaction was not as pleasant.

Carlo stared coldly at Moira, then abruptly switching to his artificial smile, he greeted her: *"Buon giorno."* Turning to Tracey, he excused himself: "I'll meet you outside."

Feeling as if he had struck her physically, Moira watched him stride away, stopping to speak to guests on the wide staircase as he went upstairs.

"Well, what's new?" Tracey asked absently, as she reached in her purse for cigarettes. "Now that he's gone, I can smoke," she added with a grin.

"Are you needing the car today?"

"Nope. You want it?" Tracey asked in surprise, pausing with the cigarette halfway to her lips. "What's the big event?"

"I thought I'd take a drive. I've nothing else to do," Moira explained, conscious of her pounding heart as she withheld her real objective.

Tracey shrugged, tossing her blonde hair. "Okay, but be careful — these roads are the dickens. It's like driving on a roller coaster. Don't tell Carlo, though. I don't think he'd be crazy about me subletting his car."

Moira agreed that it would be better not to say anything about her borrowing the car, and accepting the keys from Tracey, she went to her room to change.

Last night she had bought a map from the lobby and studied the surrounding country, choosing the best road to Blanca. It was in the mountains, and the prospect of the journey in a strange car over even stranger territory was not assuring.

Taking the jacket of her suit in case it turned cool during the afternoon, Moira went downstairs.

The man at the garage did not question her authority when she handed him the key. Moira agreed to have him bring the car to the entrance, hoping he could take a few minutes to explain the workings of the dashboard before she had to drive.

She walked briskly through the garden from the garages, which were concealed by a massive grape arbor, where bunches of purple grapes, frosted by moisture, swung temptingly overhead. In the hot afternoon the arbor formed a welcome tunnel of shade, but the morning clamminess made her welcome the warm sun dappling the broad, adjoining terrace with pools of gold.

As she neared the castello Moira saw Bettina walking toward Carlo, who was seated at a table, the morning paper propped against his coffee cup. Gasping aloud, Moira desperately sought a place to hide, not relishing a confrontation with either of them. The arbor offered little concealment. A trellis of pink roses caught her eye, and sprinting forward, she hid behind it as Bettina mounted the shallow flight of terrace steps. Moira tried to squeeze out of sight against the wall, thankful that her pink dress blended with the roses. Perhaps they would be too occupied with their own affairs to notice her. Hoping she would not sneeze from the pollen-laden air, Moira brushed against the trellis, gasping as thorns pricked her arm.

Carlo had risen from the table, and though she could not see his face, Moira knew what his expression would be. The knowledge made her stomach pitch, but it was not with pleasure.

He only spoke Bettina's name, but the emotion conveyed in his voice made Moira huddle against the wall in silent misery. She knew that her reaction was jealousy, yet he had never promised romance. A deeper meaning behind his affection was of her own construction.

Bettina answered as the tap of her heels on the stone-flagged terrace stopped.

Then Carlo exclaimed, "*Dio!* Where did you get that?"

Straining to look through the foliage, Moira gasped with surprise. For the second time she was staring at Elspeth's cross, the jasper pale yellow in the sunlight. Bettina was wearing gray slacks and a white scoop-necked top, the Celtic cross attractive against her tanned throat.

Bettina's hand flew to her neck, and she fingered the heavy cross. "Don't you like it? The stones match my shoes."

"I don't care what they match. Take it off! I hate it."

"All right, if you're going to be angry," she pouted, unhooking the clasp. "I can't see why it matters to you."

"Give it to me."

She dropped the jewelry in his outstretched hand, and Carlo studied the back of the cross before putting it in his pocket. "Did Sergio give you this?" he demanded, his hand tight around Bettina's wrist. "Don't lie to me."

"I've no intention of lying. I bought it myself. Of course, if you're going to make such an issue of it . . ."

"*Bought it?* That's impossible!"

Anger flashed across her face. "Are you calling me a liar?"

"Where did you buy it?"

"*Caro,* how can I remember? Some little town near the border — I don't recall," Bettina explained, stroking Carlo's hair, her smile inviting. "Let's not quarrel over such a silly thing."

"You are sure it was not from Sergio?" he repeated.

"Positive. He has never even seen it. Sergio isn't interested in old secondhand junk."

"Very well. I apologize," Carlo said, throwing off his anger. "Come, let us go for that sail."

He turned toward the trellis, a frown drawing his brows to heavy black lines almost concealing his eyes, and Moira realized that the incident was not so lightly forgotten. This piece of jewelry was important to Carlo, and not just because it had belonged to Elspeth. Though Bettina said that Sergio would not be interested in the cross, judging by Carlo's concern, Moira knew that the whereabouts of this particular piece of "junk" would be of vital importance to his brother.

Racing to her room, Moira studied a map of the district, concentrating on the skiing area where Elspeth had been killed. There must be a connection between the cross and Elspeth's accident. The jewelry could have been stolen by someone who had rifled Elspeth's possessions before the police arrived, or perhaps Bettina had

lied when she said that she had bought it. Whatever the answer, Moira was sure that when she
solved this mystery, the solution to other puzzling incidents would fall into place.

A rap on the door made her leap, and she
folded the map to hide that telltale portion of the
country. Only the maid waited on the threshold,
an armful of towels thrust before her.

"I thought you were out, signorina," the girl
apologized in confusion. "I will come back."

"No, it's all right," Moira assured her, an idea
forming in her mind. "I'm going shopping.
Maybe you can help me."

"*Si,* in Santa Maria?"

"No, I don't mean in town."

"Oh? Where then, signorina?" the girl asked,
her round brown eyes studying the map on the
bed as she folded towels.

"I know it's not the season, but I'm going to
the ski country and I wanted to buy a trinket for
a friend. She likes old jewelry, not valuable but
attractive."

"Sorry, I not know the shops. My cousin has a
shop in Fiori, but it not for tourist. It very poor,
his village, sometime he loan money. How you
say?"

"A pawnshop?" Moira supplied with excitement. That was a likely place for a servant to dispose of something of value. "Show me where
Fiori is."

"Here. Alfio is the only one. But you find
nothing there for your friend."

Moira was not listening. In dismay she stared at where the girl pointed, her stubby brown finger obscuring the names of the surrounding villages. Fiori was within a few kilometers of Blanca, where Elspeth had been killed — it was there, in fact, that her cousin was buried. Moira remembered the name from a letter that had accompanied Elspeth's belongings. Could Alfio's shop be where Bettina had bought the cross?

"Shops may be closed for Sunday," the maid added as she walked outside. "Not to promise, signorina."

"That's all right, thank you anyway. I'll take a chance," Moira replied, her own statement reminding her unhappily of Elspeth's favorite phrase. This whole business was beginning to weigh on her mind.

The garageman gave Moira a perfunctory course in operating *Il Conte*'s car, the title jarring on her nerves. It was bad enough having to drive the thing, its infuriating knobs and dials all in the wrong places, without being reminded that it belonged to him, she thought in annoyance, squealing to a halt at the foot of the hill to allow a couple dressed in Sunday finery to cross the road.

Instead of taking the road to Blanca, Moira turned toward Fiori, cursing the road and its treacherous bends, hoping she knew where the essential safety devices were in case of an emergency. The car had good brakes, something for which she was thankful, as she seemed to need them every few minutes.

When at last she reached Fiori, Moira discovered that every building was shuttered. The silent town, clustered precariously along steep streets, lay sleeping. It was an eerie sensation to walk the cobbled streets and meet no one, to hear no voices or traffic. Though she had grown to expect this afternoon lull, today, preoccupied by her own detective work, she had forgotten siesta.

It would be at least an hour before the businesses reopened — If they do, she added gloomily, remembering that this was Sunday. Moira glanced in the shop windows, trying to kill time. Almost guiltily she read the bright-colored posters advertising skiing in the area. What a waste to be so close to Austria and Yugoslavia and not visit the sights. Worse than that, she was close to Venice, a city tourists broke their necks to visit, and she did not intend to spend one day there. It was such a waste when she might never come back.

Turning from the window, Moira quickened her pace. Why didn't she forget this errand? Why didn't she let things rest as her own good sense suggested, instead of searching for a mystery where perhaps none existed? But Moira knew that her bond with Elspeth had been too strong to let things rest. She must learn the truth.

At the end of the street stood a gate set in a low rock wall, almost hidden by overhanging branches of a pink flowering tree. The gate stood ajar, and curiosity leading her forward, Moira pushed it open, wondering where the worn dirt path led. Then, looking over a wall of clipped cypress, she knew where she was: Fiori cemetery.

Recoiling in shocked surprise, Moira stopped on the path, knowing from what she shrank. This was where Elspeth was buried. Somewhere in that maze of white crosses stood her grave. Though she had not known before coming here, Moira discovered that the Italian custom was to adorn the crosses with photographs of the deceased. Here amongst the riotous color of flowers nestled memories of the Marias and the Giovannis of Fiori's past, their photographs a clearer reminder than any plain marble slab.

"Can I be of help, signorina?"

The voice made Moira jump. So engrossed had she been in studying these strange graves that footsteps behind her had gone unnoticed. Turning, she found an old, stooped man, his heavy thatch of white hair gleaming in the sunlight.

"Do you work here?"

"*Si*. You are looking for someone?"

"Yes, my cousin."

His face, leathery and brown, crinkled in a smile of sympathy. "I know all the graves. What is the name?"

"Breen. Elspeth Breen."

Though he made no comment, the heavy lids

of his eyes were drawn down, and his mouth, which had been kind, became straight and impersonal. With a knobby fist he indicated a small section of land set apart from the others, then he shuffled back to a stone hut shaded beneath the branches of a tree.

Puzzled by his change of attitude, Moira walked toward the graves. Here there were no pictures, only plain white crosses, and Elspeth's grave was the only one that bore fresh flowers. The bar of the cross simply stated the name, with neither birth date nor date of death. The starkness of those words gave Moira a chill. Was this deserted place amid the lovingly tended plots all they had done for Elspeth?

When she reached the old man's hut, Moira rapped sharply on the door. Cocking one eye open, he rocked forward on his chair, sighing at the disturbance. "You found the one?" he inquired, creaking to his feet.

"Why is it so neglected?"

"Neglected?" he repeated in surprise. "There are flowers. The grass is tended. It is not neglected, signorina."

"But there's no picture of her, no date."

The old man smiled, a knowing look replacing the smile as he shrugged with the eloquence of all Italians. "Those pictures are of the dead. Go home. Let her rest."

"But she *is* dead. We were told that the arrangements were made according to local custom at her own request. I can't believe she

116

asked for this," Moira protested, aware of his waning interest.

Again he shrugged. "Do the dead speak?" he asked, turning away. "The sisters bring flowers. I ask nothing. It is not my place. Some things are better left, signorina."

With this he returned to his chair, settling among the dirty cushions, and he tilted a battered felt hat over his face. By his actions Moira realized that their conversation was at an end. Whatever else he knew, she would learn no more today.

After a few minutes of baffled waiting, during which she was completely ignored, Moira retraced her steps to the gate, barely noticing the orderly rows of markers on the journey. Whatever the old man had meant to imply escaped her, yet the discovery of this added mystery only compounded her unease. Why did the sisters bring flowers to this grave? Who sent them? And why?

When she noticed signs of life in Alfio's shop, Moira went to the door and rapped on the glass. The striped blinds had gone up over the windows, but behind them no one was stirring. After what seemed an eternity, a small, dapper man opened the door, looking her over with surprise.

"Were you waiting long?" he asked, once formal greetings had been exchanged.

"Yes. I wanted to ask you some questions," Moira replied, coming inside the dusty shop and closing the door. The odor of Alfio's noon meal lingered in the air, stale garlic and wine mingling unpleasantly with the smell of secondhand clothes and musty books.

"You are from the police?" he asked with suspicion, the polite smile disappearing from his face.

"No, of course not. I want to ask about something a friend bought some time ago. I wondered if you remembered," Moira said, knowing that if he thought she were here in an official capacity she would learn nothing.

"Ah, yes." Alfio let out a sigh of relief. Turning on a light at the rear of the shop, he came back to the counter, a smile of expectancy lighting his thin face. "Now, what is it I can help you with, signorina?"

"My friend bought an old cross from you — a heavy one set with amber-colored stones. She was wondering if you could get some earrings to match, or a ring," Moira explained, her words tumbling out in a rush. She hoped she did not seem too excited.

Alfio stared blankly at her and shook his head. "I do not remember such a cross."

"But you must! I've never seen another like this. Let me draw it for you."

Shrugging, he obliged with a piece of paper and a pencil. With shaking hand Moira sketched the Celtic cross, closing her eyes to recall the exact placement of the stones. When she looked up, Alfio was regarding her intently.

"You must have the wrong shop, signorina. I

have never sold a cross like that."

Once more Moira realized that this was to be the end of the conversation. Alfio continued to smile politely, but their communication was cut. He obviously remembered, but had been sworn to silence.

"Are there any other shops like this in Fiori?" she asked.

"No, signorina."

"Perhaps in the next village?" Moira suggested.

He shook his head. "Your friend was mistaken. She bought this cross somewhere else, in the valley or across the border, but not here."

As Moira turned to go, he reached in the display case beneath the counter. "I have these earrings — very nice, cheap. Perhaps she would like these."

But Moira shook her head and pushing open the door, she walked into the hot sunshine, conscious of Alfio's penetrating brown eyes boring into her back as she moved away. He came to stand in the doorway, watching till she was out of sight.

With thudding heart Moira leaned against an arched portico leading to a small storefront, wondering what to do next. They were both hiding something, yet what could an old gravedigger have in common with Alfio, or indeed what connection could either of them have with Elspeth?

"Signorina, perhaps I can be of help."

A suave, carefully dressed man stood in the doorway. He held a wide-brimmed hat as if he had been about to go outside.

"No, I'm just lost and tired," she mumbled, wishing he would leave her alone. Strange men seemed to make a beeline for her lately.

"Allow me to introduce myself," the man continued, bowing over his hand. "I am Emilio Letti, chief of police."

Moira gulped in surprise. It seemed too much of a coincidence that she had stopped outside the local police station. Can I confide in him? she wondered, as he smiled his fixed, cardboard smile.

"I'm Moira Connor, and I'm staying in Santa Maria. Could you spare a few minutes? There's something I want to discuss."

"My time is yours, signorina," he assured, beckoning her inside an office, where a gray cat gave her a bored appraisal and then stalked haughtily toward the sunny window.

"Now, what is it?"

Though he was outwardly attentive, Moira sensed that the Fiori police chief did not take her complaints about the stolen jewelry seriously, nor, for that matter, anything else concerning Elspeth's death.

"Of course we will make inquiries, signorina. I assure you, Alfio has a reputation for honesty," Emilio Letti said, escorting her to the door. "If there is a mystery surrounding the item, it will be cleared up this very afternoon. You have my word."

"If it's possible, I don't want the owner of the cross questioned. I don't want to alert her if there's cause for suspicion," Moira insisted, pausing in the doorway of the small police station, where an overhead fan whirred lazily in the sultry afternoon.

"Naturally we will be discreet," he assured her, treating her to an indulgent smile, his clipped moustache flickering on his upper lip.

Though it seemed that she had little choice Moira was sorry she had confided her discovery to the Italian police. While he pretended dedication to his work, Moira did not completely trust him. It could be that he was involved in the entire dealing and was merely placating her with promises of help. Policemen here were different from those at home. The friendly constable of Ireland was not duplicated by his Italian counterpart.

"You might even find, dear signorina, that your cousin sold the trinket herself. Sometimes those sales became necessary. An unlucky evening at the casino, perhaps."

"No, I'm positive Elspeth wouldn't sell the cross."

"Of course, dear signorina, of course," he agreed, walking toward the door. "Enjoy your holiday. Don't let worries like this spoil your pleasure — after all, there are solutions to all things."

Hovering in the doorway, he gave Moira the impression he was waiting only for her departure to take flight on another, more exciting matter.

"Will you let me know?"

"Most certainly," he agreed.

When Moira left she watched him walking rapidly down the street in the opposite direction to Alfio's pawnshop. So much for that, she thought.

It had been dusty on the journey, and her throat was like sandpaper. She found a roadside cafe already open for business. The only other customer was an old man who accompanied the waiter when he brought her lemonade. The old man spoke English, and as their conversation progressed, she suspected he had struck up the acquaintance to show off his skill. Moira told him about her vacation, while he recounted at great length local births and marriages, and, as old men often do, the funerals of his friends.

Seizing the opportunity, Moira primed him about the famous model who had been killed at Blanca. Eager to be the center of attention, he launched into a lurid account of the accident. When he was finished and the details were permanently etched in her mind, so that when she looked toward the sloping green valley she could picture everything vividly, Moira told him that Elspeth had been her cousin.

His shock was apparent, and she regretted making him feel uncomfortable. "It's all right," she assured.

"So sorry, signorina, I did not know," he apologized, his wrinkled face expressing concern. "If you had told me . . . but so many tourists ask."

"I wanted to know how it really happened," she whispered.

"She was such a light, tiny thing."

His words broke through Moira's thoughts and in surprise she repeated: "Tiny? You saw her?"

"Not until the funeral. The coffin was the lightest I have ever carried. My brother Luca is the gravedigger."

Brooding, Moira reviewed his words. Elspeth had been willow slim, but she had also been five feet, ten inches and large boned. They had always joked about their difference in height. "The long and short of it," the girls at school had jokingly called them.

"Did you actually see my cousin's body?"

"The coffin was already sealed; as you can understand, signorina, a fall from that height . . ." He lapsed into silence, his gnarled face forming a smile of sympathy as she glanced away.

Certain facts did not add up. The newspaper accounts had revealed that Elspeth had disappeared from the hospital before the specialist summoned from Milan had arrived. Her subsequent death had been followed by a quiet funeral with closed coffin, the location of the grave kept secret until afterward. Now this.

"Do you think I could visit the doctor who

signed the death certificate? Would he remember?" she asked, putting on her sunglasses.

"Such a tragedy is not easy to forget. I will give you his address."

In a few minutes Moira was behind the wheel of the small sports car, driving along the narrow road and trying not to look at the precipice below. When she eventually reached the huddled streets of Blanca, clinging precariously to the mountainous terrain, many buildings were still shuttered for the afternoon.

After a twenty-minute search along rocky streets, she located the doctor's house from the scrawled map the old man had drawn for her. There on a brass plate set in the pink stone wall beside the door was the word *Dottore*. At least it was one word of Italian she could translate.

The household seemed to be asleep. After knocking persistently for several minutes, Moira was rewarded by the echo of footsteps. The blue-painted door opened a couple of inches, and a middle-aged woman peered out. Her hawklike face was dark, her high-bridged nose curving like a beak. After a moment, when her beady black eyes were satisfied, she said, "It is still siesta, signorina. Please to come back later."

She spoke halting English, and Moira wondered how the servant knew that she was not Italian — unless she had been alerted to expect her.

"The *dottore*, may I see him?" Moira blurted,

afraid the woman would close the door.

"You are ill?"

"No, not that. I want to speak to him about a patient."

"He is not here. Please to come back later." And the door was closed in her face.

Though Moira banged on the door, the footsteps steadfastly retreated, until her own voice echoed in the silent street. Wondering what to do next, she leaned against the sun-baked wall, wiping her hand over her brow, where her hair trailed, sticky and sweaty.

A blaring horn shattered the quiet as a small red car swerved around the corner, skidding to a halt beside her. It was Carlo.

"What happened, run out of petrol?" he asked, indicating the car parked under the shade of the overhanging trees.

"How did you know where I was?" Moira gasped, taken aback by his unexpected appearance, but more shocked to hear him speak to her as if nothing were wrong between them.

"Would you believe I have spies?" He laughed, disentangling his long body from the seat of the car.

Moira laughed, too, wondering if there might be more than a little truth to his statement. Whatever his reason for following her, it had prompted this show of cordiality. Well, she thought, two can play this game.

"Spies I'll overlook," she said dismissing it nonchalantly. "How did you really know?"

"Sergio's assistant told me you had driven this way. Did you learn what you wanted to know?"

"I wasn't trying to learn anything," Moira replied, her heart missing a beat.

"Why did you want to speak to the *dottore* then?"

She hesitated, glancing helplessly about the deserted street, wishing something would distract him from demanding an answer to his question. But the street remained empty.

"Well?" he reminded, stepping closer.

"It's natural to want to talk to the doctor who attended an injured relative."

"You lie so prettily, Moira — I wish to God I could believe you." He gripped her wrist until she thought that he would crush the bones.

"Please! You're hurting me," she gasped, trying to pull free.

"Why are you really here?" Carlo demanded, slackening the pressure slightly. "I want to know who you are working for."

"I'm not working for anyone."

Abruptly he dropped her wrist. "Have it your way."

"I'm waiting till they open the door," Moira vowed. "I mean to see him."

Carlo snorted in scorn. "Very well, if you insist. We shall both be made wiser."

This was not what Moira wanted, but it seemed that she had no choice. With him beside her it would be impossible to ask any questions that could implicate either of the brothers.

"You don't have to wait. That's all right."

"But I insist."

He came to the door and rang the bell. Almost at once the door was opened, making Moira suspect that the servant had been listening.

"Signorina . . . ah, *Signor il Conte.*" Scrambling to a bob of obeisance, the woman turned her attention to Carlo.

"*Buona sera,* Magdela. Tell this young lady why your master cannot come to the door. She had an idea she will learn some dire secret from him."

Moira drew back, annoyed by the jesting manner in which he referred to her suspicions. The woman hesitated; then, encouraged by his reassuring nod, she directed her piercing black eyes toward Moira.

"I am very sorry, signorina. The *dottore* is dead."

Her words were such a shock that Moira gasped her indignant thoughts aloud: "I don't believe you!"

Carlo shrugged. "I should have known. Did you spend all your time reading mystery novels?"

Glaring at him, Moira ignored his sarcasm, speaking instead to the servant. "Why didn't you tell me that before? You said to come back later."

Magdela's bronzed face could have been carved from wood for all the expression it bore. Only her black eyes were alive.

"Come on, there's nothing more for you here," Carlo said, drawing Moira toward the car after the door had been closed by the hostile servant. "A dead man can tell you nothing."

His words struck chill through her body, prickling down her back and across her arms. His questions about her purpose for being here and about working for someone made Moira even more suspicious of the handsome conte. And that sentence, delivered so finally, increased her feeling that Carlo was more involved in Elspeth's death than she wanted to admit. The thought was frightening, and at once Moira rejected it. When he smiled at her, offering his hand to assist her into the car, he was devastatingly charming. How could Carlo be involved in anything criminal? she asked herself as she started the engine, pushing those disturbing thoughts to the back of her mind.

Carlo leaned over the windshield, his scarlet shirt a bright patch through the glass. "I'm sorry for yesterday, for my bad manners."

"But not for your anger?"

He shrugged at her question. "No, my anger was justified. Now I want you to follow me to Santa Maria. It's safer that way."

Smarting in annoyance at his manner, Moira wanted to squeal away, passing him on the narrow road and making it impossible for him to lead the way, but her innate good sense squelched the thought. Instead she waited while he manuevered his sports car back onto the main road and motioned her to follow.

He drove slowly, making the return journey less of a nightmare for her. Before they reached Santa Maria she discovered with dismay that she had all but forgiven him. None of that! she thought with a determined frown. Being polite was one thing, being a foolish doormat was something else.

Instead of driving to the castello, Carlo turned toward the beach, parking his car outside the colorful bay-front shops.

"It's early. Let me take you to a little place on the waterfront. They have delicious cassata," Carlo persuaded, ignoring her lame objections.

"All right, but only for a few minutes. I must get back," Moira reminded him with a smile. Though she could not tell him, she was awaiting that reply from Fiori, if it came at all. From Emilio Letti's manner this morning, the latter was quite possible that it would not.

"I don't even know what cassata is," she confided when they were seated in a secluded corner of the restaurant. The tables were covered with red checked cloths, and multicolored candles stuck in straw-covered wine bottles provided romantic lighting. Fishermen's nets were draped about the dark walls, which seemed to be hewn from solid rock, brightened by fluorescent, glowing seashells and a lifelike plastic octopus that jiggled in the breeze.

"You will see. It's very rich and bad for the figure, but yours won't be affected," he assured her huskily, treating her to a sweeping glance of appraisal.

His approval made Moira flush with pleasure, despite her earlier resolution to be no more than polite.

Cassata was a huge slice of iced cream cake filled with chunks of crystallized fruit and nuts. It was delicious, but before she was halfway through with the gigantic slice, Moira began to stall — in Italy a slice always seemed to mean almost a quarter of the cake.

It was already dark when they arrived at the hotel. Moira had been lulled into a state of happiness by Carlo's apparent forgiveness.

"There is a telegram for you, signorina," the desk man greeted her as she walked into the lobby. "Oh, *Signor il Conte,* a thousand pardons," he apologized, seeing that she was not alone, "but perhaps it is urgent."

Carlo smiled in understanding, lighting a cigarette while he waited. "Well, open it," he urged, as Moira hesitated, wishing she could have been alone to read this important message.

"Yes, of course," she agreed, opening the envelope with shaking hands, tearing and crumpling the paper in her agitation. Her hands trembled as she withdrew the thin paper, conscious of the amused scrutiny of Carlo's brown eyes as he leaned against the reception desk.

The message burned in her brain: "Receipt obtained. Signature E. Breen. Description unknown." The telegram was signed "Emilio

Letti, Fiori chief of police." He had immediately gone to work on her complaint, after all, she thought with dawning relief.

Becoming conscious of Carlo's questioning expression, Moira crumpled the paper and casually explained, "It's just confirming my return reservation. Everything's all right."

"I see."

As she smiled at him, Moira realized that Carlo did not believe a word she said. Instinct told her this, for nothing was betrayed in his face as he proffered his arm. And though she allowed him to lead her to the brightly lit bar, Moira squirmed in discomfort at the knowledge. Things were not the same between them after all.

Chapter 8

Only one week left, Moira thought sadly on Monday morning as she peered beneath the frayed edge of the brocade curtains, surprised to find the day overcast. For once the sparkling sunshine had been replaced by a ceiling of clouds. It seemed months since she had boarded the jet for Italy; it was impossible to believe it was only seven days ago.

The phone rang, and she jumped, startled by the unexpected noise. The early caller was Tracey, inviting her for a dip in the pool.

While they swam Moira reviewed yesterday's visit to Blanca. She wondered if someone had really told Carlo where she was or if he had lied to her. The condition of Elspeth's grave combined with the old man's recollection of the lightness of the coffin puzzled her. Could someone else be buried in her place? Had she not simply stumbled on Elspeth's murder, but perhaps uncovered a double crime? Or, on the other hand, perhaps she was making a mystery out of perfectly normal events.

Though Tracey could not overlook Moira's distraction, she allowed her the luxury of undisturbed thought. "Say, did you get back together with Carlo?" she asked when their swim was over, levering herself over the edge of the blue-tiled swimming pool.

Moira joined her, dabbling her toes in the clear water. "There's nothing between us," she explained quietly, forcing a casual tone to her voice, though even speaking about him set her heart racing. To make her nonchalance more convincing, she lazily applied suntan lotion before stretching out on a webbed lounge chair beside Tracey.

"Sorry, I thought perhaps you'd quarreled or something."

"A disagreement, that's all."

Tracey's throaty chuckle made Moira flush, for she knew exactly what the other girl suspected about the nature of their quarrel.

"It wasn't about that," Moira defended, finding it necessary to set the record straight.

"You don't have to try to convince me. Remember, I knew him first!" Tracey laughed, slipping her arm across Moira's slick shoulders. "Anyway, how'd the sight-seeing turn out yesterday?"

"It was fun."

"Where'd you go?"

"Just around the countryside. The mountains were pretty, and it was a lot cooler, too."

But Tracey was not listening as she hunted through her drawstring bag. "You should be careful — those roads are bad," she said over her shoulder, spilling the contents of her bag on a metal poolside table.

"I drove slowly," Moira defended, surprised by her abruptness.

When Tracey turned around, her face was drawn, the usual sophisticate replaced by a harried, frightened woman. "Here's the book I was telling you about. Take it."

To her surprise, Moira found a book thrust in her hands, while Tracey scrambled to her feet, haphazardly sweeping her belongings into her beach bag. Moira remembered discussing reading materials several days ago, but Tracey had definitely not offered her a book.

"So long, I'll talk to you later. Look after it." Tracey ran between the poolside tables, lost to view in seconds behind the tilting, bright-striped umbrellas on the terrace.

"My dear, dear, Miss Connor."

With sinking heart Moira saw Mr. Bear. That was why Tracey had dashed away — she must have seen him walking around the other side of the pool. What luck! There was no escape. She would just have to stay and be polite.

"Hello. Did you enjoy the show yesterday?" she asked, managing a slightly frosty smile.

Eagerly Mr. Bear maneuvered onto the lounge chair beside her, the stuffed plastic seat sagging between the metal slats under his bulk. "I missed you, baby."

Wanting to tell him that she was definitely not his "baby," Moira maintained her composure, pointedly removing his flaccid hand when it came to rest on her bare shoulder.

"I had business elsewhere, as I have this morning," she ended on an inspiration, scrambling to her feet.

But he was too fast. "Oh, no, baby, not twice. Today you stay and have a drink with me. Just one," he pleaded, his shiny red face taking on an unbecoming cherubic pose as he pursed his thick lips.

Not knowing how to leave without being rude, Moira reluctantly agreed to a drink. But she was careful to sit as far from him as she could, uncomfortably conscious of the pressure of his knee against hers. After what seemed an eternity the waiter brought their drinks. Mr. Bear had a brandy, while Moira ordered lime juice, wishing later she had not done so, for her order met with a chortle of glee from Mr. Bear, who made tasteless jokes about Limeys.

Consuming the limeade in record time, Moira made her exit with determination, even though he became his gross, cherubic self in an effort to cajole her into going to town with him for the evening film.

After firmly wishing him good-day, Moira gathered her belongings and headed for her room. Mr. Bear was becoming a menace. In the future she would have to keep her eyes open, as Tracey had obviously done. Fortunately she had never needed to address him by name, for he was still Mr. Bear to her. To have requested an introduction would only have spurred his interest.

On the way past Tracey's room, Moira

knocked on the door, intending to return the book and demand an explanation for her friend's hasty actions. There was no reply. When she tried the handle she found the door locked. Maybe Tracey was taking a bath. After lunch would be time enough to ask about that cloak-and-dagger stuff at the pool.

When she had changed from her wet suit, Moira took the paperback book from her beach bag, wondering if the modest jacket were only a sham concealing more exciting information. To her disappointment she found it to be exactly as promised: a detective novel.

As the guests filed in to lunch, Carlo joined her in the entrance to the dining hall, politely offering his arm, an unexpected gesture that pleased and surprised her. Was he willing to forget the island quarrel after all? Though she looked for Tracey among the seated guests, Moira did not see her, which was disconcerting. Despite her slim figure, Tracey never missed a meal. And Moira could not help wondering uneasily if Tracey's hasty departure this morning was responsible for her absence.

"I'm sorry for being so angry with you. I don't think you accepted my apology yesterday," Carlo murmured.

Not expecting this admission, Moira stared down at her steaming plate of salmon risotto and fumbled for words. To have Carlo ready to begin where they had left off had been one of her fondest dreams since they had quarreled at the villa, one she had repeatedly tried to squelch. Now that he was apologizing, rewarding her with his melting brown eyes, Moira was not sure she wanted to begin again. If he had come to her the very next morning with an apology, she would not have hesitated; but so much had happened since, events that warned her to view his attentions warily.

"Come on, don't keep me in suspense," he urged, resting his fingers lightly against the back of her hand.

"I accept your apology," she mumbled, shivering at his touch. There was now a nagging reminder of her cousin behind their meetings, as if Elspeth hovered in the shadows, warning her not to repeat her own fatal mistake. Was Carlo aware that she had seen Elspeth's cross, or was he hiding it in the hope she would never learn of its existence? An idea charged her brain, her reason supplying an excuse for becoming involved with him again. If Carlo still had the cross, there might be a chance to examine it and learn what he had seen on the back, the secret he had not wanted Sergio to discover.

"I believed you yesterday," she forced herself to add, ignoring the pang of guilt she felt at his apparent delight.

"That's a relief." He laughed, tension lifting from his face. "You know, Moira, it's foolish to keep old memories alive. They're far better buried with the dead."

It was only when she lay in her room relaxing during the afternoon heat that Moira remembered that the Campella collection would be gone tomorrow. And with it, Bettina.

Disappointment flooded achingly to her throat, robbing her of the pleasure she had felt when she dreamily relived the warmth of his parting kiss. That was why Carlo was so anxious to make up. With Bettina gone, why not string Moira along for a few days till someone better showed up? Knowing Carlo, he may still be hoping for a conquest, Moira conceded miserably, licking the tears that trickled to the corners of her mouth. Of all the nerve! And she had been stupid enough to fall right in with his plans. As a conquest she was probably as challenging and exciting as an old-maid missionary. Even the reminder of the purpose behind their relationship — to get the cross — could not erase her disappointment.

Thumping her pillow in anger, Moira leaped from the bed. She would find Tracey and find out what the episode at the pool had been about. At least it would take her mind off Carlo.

The door was still locked, and there was no answer to her knock. Thinking Tracey might be asleep, Moira banged louder, determined to rouse her. She waited several minutes in the deserted corridor for some reply, until, in panic, she saw Mr. Bear puffing upstairs carrying a suitcase. Hoping he had not seen her, Moira raced back to her own room. Reaching her door safely, she nearly fell inside, gasping with relief as she latched the door; and though she listened uneasily for his heavy steps, there was no sound.

Retiring to the luxury of her bed, Moira picked up Tracey's detective novel, and though the first chapter was interesting enough, she began to nod, finally making use of the siesta.

The afternoon quiet was shattered by the hysterical screams of Mrs. Wilburn Kay as she ran down the hotel corridor shrieking, "My diamonds are gone. I've been robbed! Don't just stand there, Wilburn, *do* something!"

Mr. Kay's reply was drowned by his wife's anguished wails. The thud of running footsteps went past the door, accompanied by many excited voices jabbering in rapid Italian. While Moira was hastily dressing to go outside to investigate, there came a rap on her door.

"Signorina Connor, so sorry to trouble you." Mario stood outside, his face lined with worry, for his duties as desk clerk had temporarily been extended to those of house detective. "Have you missed any valuables?"

"No, I don't really have any." Moira laughed in apology. "But I'll see if everything's here."

At Mario's nod of agreement, she scanned the contents of her handbag, finding her passport, the keys to her cases, and her wallet still there.

"Nothing missing."

"A thousand pardons. Just routine." Mario excused himself, his face brightening. "*Buona sera,* signorina."

After he had left, Moira slipped her handbag under the clothes in the dressing-table drawer. Any self-respecting thief would check the drawers, but there was a little comfort in the saying, "Out of sight, out of mind." In all probability her room would not be touched. A few thousand lire and a British passport were not worth the risk involved.

"How terrible that the contessa's jewels were stolen," Moira said sympathetically when Carlo escorted her to the terrace after dinner.

"News travels fast," he snapped, his face in shadow. "But I'd forgotten — the display case is empty. Anyone can see that."

"You could always have put them in the safe," Moira reminded him, puzzled by his lack of emotion over the theft. For a man in dire financial need, the loss of his family heirlooms seemed to have little effect. "I suppose you could even have sold them," she suggested lightly, unprepared for his violent reaction.

Carlo spun toward her, his hand gripping her arm like a vise. "What?"

"I was only joking! I don't care what you did with them."

"Never joke about that — if it *was* a joke," he warned, his mouth set in an angry line.

"Now, I'm not suggesting you're the thief or anything like that," Moira apologized, alarmed at the anger in his face. It had been pleasanter when she could not see the hardness of his eyes. "After all, they are valuable, and you told me the hotel was losing money."

"Those jewels are never sold, they are inherited," Carlo explained shortly. "Do not suggest such a thing again. If the wrong people heard, they could make things difficult."

"I'm sorry. I know what a strain this must have been."

The pressure on her arm slackened, and the smile returned to Carlo's face. He was once more the perfect host, the handsome conte, yet Moira could not forget the fear his suspicion evoked in her.

Though Carlo danced with her, Moira sensed the anger behind his forced charm. Her blurted words over the contessa's jewels had brought back his flashing temper. Their entire relationship was becoming impossibly stormy, she decided when halfway through the evening he excused himself to make a phone call. After waiting thirty minutes for his return, Moira decided to wait no longer. A headache, pressing like an iron band on her brow, made the music and chatter unbearable. A jewel theft added to the already baffling situation was too much.

When she passed Tracey's room, Moira found the door open and Tracey packing a suitcase on the bed. "Are you leaving?" Moira cried in disappointment, wondering at the sudden departure.

Tracey leaped visibly, Moira's appearance

coming as a shock. "Oh, hi! I thought you were still dancing with Carlo."

"I was, but he had to take a phone call. Are you leaving now?"

"Not till tomorrow. Oh, my God! What's that?" Tracey cried as a loud clap of thunder rattled the windows.

"It's only a storm brewing. I saw lightning from the terrace," Moira supplied, surprised by Tracey's unusually nervous reaction. The other girl was always such a rock of assurance that something really traumatic must have happened to upset her like this. "I thought you weren't leaving till the end of the week. Is it bad news?"

"Just a change of plans." Tracey dismissed it shortly. "By the way, that book I gave you — I'd like it back."

"That's what I've been wanting to ask you about." Moira smiled, coming to perch on the edge of the bed while Tracey methodically folded nylon lingerie.

"Guess I was kind of melodramatic," Tracey stalled, careful not to look up.

"Well, you left me in a situation all right. That Mr. Bear drives me up the pole."

"Mr. Bear? Who's he?"

Half apologetically Moira laughed. "Well, that's not really his name, but he never introduced himself, thank goodness. The fat man in the gray suit who sat next to me at the show. You must have seen him. He was the only one at that table who wasn't in costume."

To her surprise, Moira saw Tracey pale, her eyes dilated with fear. "What have you told him?" she demanded.

"Told him? What do you mean?"

"Come on, Moira, stop pretending. I know all about you."

With a gulp Moira repeated, "All about me?"

"Why you came here."

"I came because my cousin booked the holiday."

"Your cousin was Elspeth Breen."

Tracey's words caught her off guard, and all Moira could do was stare at her in stunned silence. Carlo was the only one who knew. Yesterday while sailing he must have revealed the whole story.

"How?" was all she managed after an uncomfortable silence.

Tracey dropped the amused smile she had assumed, her face growing taut. "Oh, you're transparent, honey. Transparent and pretty dumb. Don't ask me how I know. Just accept the fact that I do, but also realize that I'm not the only one on to you."

"*On to me!*" Moira exploded in indignation. "What on earth do you mean?"

"Well," Tracey said, "maybe 'on to you' is a bit like cops and robbers. Let me just say that if you've got any smarts in that red head, you'll leave on the first plane. There's a lot going on here you haven't the first idea about. If you did, you'd be scared to death."

It was a temptation to reveal what she already knew, but Moira kept silent. This new Tracey Cole frightened her.

"The jewel robbery . . . Is that what you mean?"

"I don't mean anything, honey. Just bring me the book, and forget I mentioned it. And stay away from Mr. Bear — cuddly and lovable, he isn't!"

Tracey went to answer the phone and Moira darted to her room to fetch the book, her mind a turmoil of unanswered questions. In the hallway she collided with Maffeo, the garageman, who helped her up with profuse apologies, though Moira knew the collison had been her own fault.

When she returned to Tracey's room, the book in her hand, Tracey had gone. The locked suitcase was on the bed where she had left it, the light was still on, but Tracey was nowhere to be seen. She could not have disappeared into thin air, Moira thought. With thudding heart Moira searched the closet and the small adjoining bathroom in the hope of finding some clues. This corridor ended at a door to the private apartments, offering no way out at that end, yet Tracey had not come past Moira's room . . . unless she had gone with Maffeo to the private apartments.

Giving no thought to the danger of exploring, Moira tried the handle on the curtained door to the north wing of the castello. To her surprise it turned in her hand, for it was unlocked. With pounding heart she slipped inside, groping along the rough stone wall. Though Carlo had brought her through this door during her tour, it was much different in the daytime. Now there was no comforting light. The passage and the rooms leading from it stood in black shadow. Rumbling thunder crashed like cymbals, and stifling a scream, Moira leaned against the cold stone, her knees going from under her in shock. After quieting her racing heart, she continued her journey, though her legs were weak and she was conscious of their nervous tremoring.

The wide gallery she reached was not familiar, and from somewhere close at hand Moira could hear men's voices. Maybe this was where they had brought Tracey. Drawing closer, she saw a wedge of light shining beneath a closed door. The bellow of a gruff voice raised in anger made her jump a second time, and she stumbled against the wall.

"You imbecile, they're paste!"

It was Sergio who spoke next, his voice shrill and angry: "*What?* It can't be true! They've been revered for centuries."

Someone stood, scraping a chair, and heavy footsteps announced the nervous pacing of the other man.

"How?" Sergio demanded, his voice rising.

"Perhaps your brother isn't the fool you took him for."

Though Moira strained to hear more, the

noise of the rolling thunder drowned their voices. Paste was imitation jewelry. Had Mrs. Kay's flashing diamonds been fakes? Then the truth rushed through her mind, taking her breath away. Sergio was not discussing Mrs. Kay's trinkets, those had only been icing on the cake; the real haul had been the contessa's jewels. Now Moira knew why Carlo had been so angry when she had suggested that he had sold them. Her theory had been too close for comfort. He must have replaced the originals with imitations, successfully deceiving the thieves.

"That money has to be somewhere."

"Then find it."

"I've tried!" Sergio cried. "Why is it my job?"

"Because you had the girl and you bungled it."

"I went over her things a thousand times. Nothing."

The other voice exploded in scornful laughter. "Now we have one million American dollars at stake, you fool, and you couldn't even solve your brother's schemes. *Gott*, I am the fool to trust you."

Moira heard them move to another room, then there was silence. She waited a couple of minutes, puzzling over the voices. Sergio's light, cultured tones she had recognized at once, but the other voice, while seeming familiar, was not as easy to place.

Following the floor plan of the castello, all these rooms should open onto a balcony facing the sea. She tried the next door in the black passage, and fortunately it was not locked. This room was shrouded in dust covers, lending strange, unreal shapes to the bulky furniture. Her heart in her mouth, she moved toward the window, where lightning flashed to illuminate the grotesque figures behind her, until she almost expected them to move, so lifelike did they appear. The catch on the French window was hard to open, but she finally managed, thunder drowning the resistant groan of the hinges.

Thunder hampered her efforts at eavesdropping as she crouched outside the windows to the next room. She could hear voices, but she could not understand the words. The conversation became louder, but to her disappointment Moira found that they had switched to a foreign language. As she strained against the cold glass, the wind whipping at her hair, she decided that they were speaking German. Three voices argued now, and a fist was pounded on a table. Cautiously she tried to peer inside the room, but the curtain was opaque and fitted too close to the windows to leave spy holes. All she could see were four shadows against the light.

"You couldn't touch them — you knew that!" Sergio yelled in English, his voice rising in near hysteria.

To her surprise Moira heard Carlo's low voice, and she leaned close to the glass to hear his reply.

"I'm sorry, there was no other way," he said.

"If you'd been patient, there would have been money for us both."

"You've said enough," someone silenced.

Movement came from inside the room, and in alarm Moira cast about for a place to hide. Carlo's voice was louder now, as if he were standing right on the other side of the window.

"Don't be so self-righteous, brother," he snarled in contempt. "Your anger stems only from being outmaneuvered. By your method I stood to lose it all."

"You've already lost, *Il Conte*," said another, the pure loathing in the tone making Moira shudder.

"We shall see," was all that Carlo said; then the window handle creaked, the latch popping up.

Moira scrambled toward the darkened room, praying she could hide behind the furniture before she was discovered. To be Elspeth's cousin was one thing; to be caught spying on a secret discussion was something quite different. And though Carlo seemed to be the odd man out, his innocence had not been established. If he thought that she had eavesdropped, he would fly into a rage. He might do more than that, she thought with racing heart, squeezing behind the dust-laden chair near the window. Though she wanted to believe that Carlo was not involved in anything illegal, Moira knew she could not deny it now, however hard she tried.

The French window clicked open, and

someone stepped inside. A flashlight went on, and Moira gasped in alarm, thinking she was discovered as the white beam swept the room. But she need not have worried. Whoever came inside was not searching for her. The light focused on a portrait opposite the window, bringing it to pulsing life. The man was Carlo; the painting was of his mother.

He swayed unsteadily, and Moira realized he had been drinking. In one hand Carlo held the flashlight, in the other, a wine bottle, which he put to his lips as he studied the painting.

Then, in a voice full of hurt and bitterness, he demanded of the painted face: "Are you proud of me, *Madre?* Now I'm truly your son — the last of the del Santa Marias. And I've kept your precious castello — shabbier, dirtier — but it still lives."

The woman's black eyes seemed to smile at him, the mouth widening in fiendish pleasure. Moira gasped at the tricks her eyes were playing, until she saw that it was only the effect of the flashlight in Carlo's unsteady hand.

"You taught me well the tenet of our faith: our tabernacle must be saved at all costs." He paused, and resting against a shrouded table, he drained the bottle.

A lump rose in Moira's throat as she listened. These words were torn from him in anguish, too private for anyone but the contessa. Whatever she personally felt about Carlo, Moira knew pity for him — or, more accurately, for that little boy revealed within the man, the child who had been spurned so long ago.

"Well, *Madre,* I grew up without you. Then I couldn't understand why you hated my father, how you could hate me because I looked like him. I still don't know, but I'm learning. You were such a good teacher. You taught me how to lie and deceive — you even tried to teach me how to kill."

Tears slid over Moira's cheeks, and she wanted to blow her nose, but dared not even sniff. With a carefree wave to the portrait, he stumbled toward the door and was gone.

The room seemed suddenly colder, and Moira was aware of a draft that passed beside her, icy and encompassing. The window to the terrace was closed, and she could not understand the frigid air. Had it been the contessa's presence following her son? The idea was preposterous, yet so was the scene that had taken place behind the iron-banded door to the private apartments of the del Santa Marias.

Chapter 9

Moira was awakened near midnight by a booming roll of thunder that rattled the door. For a few moments she lay shivering, shocked to consciousness by the deafening crash. The room was hot, for instead of cooling, the rain had only raised the humidity until the bedcovers were damp against her skin.

A walk outdoors would be pleasant, she thought wistfully, listening for rain but hearing none. At this hour the gardens would be deserted, and she could enjoy an uninterrupted stroll. Her mind made up, Moira slipped a dress over her nightgown, and carrying her shoes, she slipped quietly outside.

The storm was blowing out to sea, though the wind still shrieked like a lost soul, turning the dripping tree branches to flails, which whipped her body as she walked over the grass. Once Moira would have hesitated to go outside at night, but after Tracey's disappearance the hotel bedrooms did not seem as safe as they had once appeared.

A high, piercing note echoed in the wind, and Moira shivered at the eerie sound. Carlo had been right: it did sound like someone screaming for help. Recalling the cold air sweeping through the contessa's bedroom sent a prickle of fear along her spine. Could there be something to the legend after all? Deciding not to tempt fate, Moira retraced her steps from the shingled brink of the lake, depressed by the black, heaving water. Her mind flashed to that shrouded bedroom where Carlo had conversed with the portrait of his mother, liquor weakening the cool resolve he had displayed moments before when confronted by those threatening men. Tempted to take him into her confidence and disclose what she had learned at Blanca, Moira held back. He still kept Elspeth's cross a secret from her. Despite Emilio Letti's saying that the receipt was signed "E. Breen," she was certain Elspeth would not have parted with it. As anyone could have signed her cousin's name, Alfio would have been none the wiser.

The deep-throated voice of an engine came from the lake, and Moira scanned the water, wondering what idiot would be out on a night like this. She watched for several minutes but saw no lights. The ruined villa was suddenly illuminated by a flash of lightning, which sent the paneless windows into dark relief against the garish sky, like a dozen sightless eyes.

Moira shivered, chilled by the eerie sight and the steadily rising wind. It was time to return to the comfort of her bed, she decided, quickening her steps. And as she stifled a yawn, she was satisfied that the walk had served its purpose in readying her for sleep.

Morning heralded its arrival with the usual golden fingers of sunlight poking beneath the swagged cornice at the windows. Feeling unusually pleased with herself, Moira stretched beneath the covers, relieved to find that the storm had passed. An idea had presented itself in her drowsy waking moments. In all this bewildering muddle she had forgotten the one person who could help her, who was not involved with either Elspeth or this castello: there was still Chris.

Moira was reaching for her robe when the phone rang. Scrambling over the bed, she leaned across the pillow, picking up the ivory phone.

"Hello, Moira Connor here."

"This is Emilio Letti, Fiori chief of police."

"Yes," Moira said, her heart making lurching jumps.

"There was a drowning last night. Would you come to the hotel office? I would like to ask you some questions."

Tracey was dead. Moira was stunned by the news. Though she wanted to dispute their story, she accepted the truth, knowing that Emilio Letti or the policeman from Santa Maria would not be here otherwise. After last night's revealing scene, Carlo's presence made Moira uncomfortable. That emotion was quickly compounded when he disclosed her true identity. Though her heart was in her mouth, she was relieved when Emilio Letti acted appropriately surprised by the news. He must not have told Carlo about her visit.

"I heard a launch last night when I was in the garden," Moira remembered when their questions were finished. That midnight walk had almost merged with her dreams, but it had been real, because this morning her shoes were still wet from the rain-soaked grass.

"A launch?" the Santa Maria policeman asked. "Are you sure?"

"Yes, because I wondered what kind of idiot would be out there in the storm," Moira said remembering her reaction.

"That's strange. Signorina Cole was in a rowboat."

"But I heard an engine. It was very loud."

"Probably the wind. I told you it plays tricks around the island." Carlo laughed, but his eyes had narrowed as he studied her face. "The launch was inoperable last night. There is no other boat."

"But I heard it."

"You only thought you heard it," Carlo concluded, standing up. "The signorina has been under stress — Miss Cole was her friend." The other men nodded in sympathy.

Crossing to the cabinet beneath the window, Carlo poured three glasses of wine. This morning his eyes were bloodshot and his face haggard, his appearance reminding Moira of his drinking bout last night. Noticing his crumpled shirt, she wondered if he had slept in his clothes.

154

Had he taken the boat out and not remembered once he was sober?

"How can you be so sure I didn't hear a boat?"

"Because, my dear, the launch is in Maffeo's shed, awaiting repairs. It could not have been used last night."

Moira stared at him. Carlo was lying; he had to be. She might have imagined the contessa's ghost, but not the sound of that noisy motor launch.

"Thank you very much, Signorina Connor. I'm sorry to have to question you. The case seems clear — one of those unfortunate accidents." Emilio Letti dismissed her, indicating the door. "We won't need you any more."

Moira found herself outside in the hallway, and she heard Carlo laughing with the policemen while they sipped wine. This is unreal, she thought in dismay, listening to their carefree voices. When she had told them what she had heard, circumstantial evidence though it might be, they could at least have investigated her story. Tracey was too good a swimmer to have drowned in that lake. Whoever was in the boat had followed her to make certain that an "accident" took place. After considering telling the police about Tracey's strange behavior last night and her subsequent disappearance while waiting for the book, Moira decided against it. To admit that she knew that much could put her own life in danger. Besides, if he ran true to form, Emilio Letti would not have believed a word of the story. It was just as well that they did not know she had anything belonging to Tracey; the police would probably impound it as evidence.

Still puzzling about the drowning, Moira walked to her room. Nothing appeared to have been disturbed, and the important book lay untouched on the dressing table.

After locking the door Moira pocketed the key. The lock gave her a feeling of security. There was also a bolt on the French windows, though their flimsy structure provided little safety.

For some reason this book was highly important to Tracey, Moira thought, picking up the brightly jacketed detective mystery, determined to solve its secret. Inside the flyleaf was the name Tracey Anne Cole, followed by two phone numbers. The only other writing was a penciled note on the bottom of the last page. It was the title of a book: *Santa Maria at War*, Vol. 4, p. 25. That must be a historical note, Moira concluded, stopping to pick up Tracey's bookmark, which had fallen to the floor. Passages in a history book certainly suggested a writer, but by now that idea was too tame — much more had to be involved.

Whatever conclusion the police had made concerning Tracey's death leaned heavily on Carlo's information about the boat. Recalling his anger when she had insisted that she had heard the launch, Moira found goose bumps prickling her arms. He had been daring her to repeat her story, warning and challenge on his face. While she thought uneasily about Carlo's reaction, Moira absently rolled and unrolled the piece of paper that had been made into a bookmark. Then she gasped with surprise as she read the writing on the paper: "Must see you tonight on cypress island. Carlo."

Finding that her legs had grown weak, she plopped on the edge of the bed. Tracey had been keeping a rendezvous last night; it had not been just an impulsive act, as everyone seemed to believe. And Carlo had lied. How else could he have gone to the cypress island except by boat? Yet if he were already waiting for Tracey on shore, why had he not answered her cries for help? Perhaps *he* was the *murderer!*

This conclusion brought a wave of panic as she remembered the gentle touch of Carlo's hands on her throat. If only she had found the note this morning, she would never have told them she had heard the boat. By then the reason for his insistence that the launch was beached would have been obvious. Maffeo was in the conte's pay — what else could he say but to agree? When Moira had seen Maffeo outside Tracey's room last night he must have been coming for her at Carlo's request.

For over an hour Moira did not move from the edge of the bed, her mind going around in circles as she wondered what to do next. It would be no use to go to Tracey's room in the hope of finding some clues; whoever had caused her accident had probably taken everything. But there was still this book. The phone numbers could be traced by the operator; the passage from the history book she would find herself.

To her dismay Moira discovered that the library was in the private section of the castello. For over an hour she waited for her chance to slip through the staff entrance. The door by Tracey's room was too risky — perhaps now it was being watched.

After lunch, when the corridors had grown quiet, Moira walked unobserved through the kitchens. Before embarking on her mission, she studied a map in the lobby showing the complete floor plan of the castello. The library was located near the rooms where she had eavesdropped last night, though from the kitchen entrance she must travel through the north wing to reach it.

Moira arrived at the library without incident. There was a study off the main room, and she was careful not to make a noise until she knew that it was empty. This must be where Carlo kept his accounts. Both desk drawers and a metal file cabinet were locked. After she had found the book — if there were sufficient time — she would look for a key. Whatever was in those drawers might provide her with all the information she needed.

The books on the library shelves were thick with dust. It was a huge, gloomy room, lit by the multicolored glow from a large stained-glass window depicting haloed saints and strong, sad-faced horses. Though she would have liked to switch on the lights, Moira was afraid that action would attract attention. Close to panic over the time it took to locate the volume in the red-and-blue murk, she finally found the leather-bound series on a bottom shelf near the window.

Moira took *Santa Maria at War*, Vol. 4 closer to the window so she could read the small type. It was a privately printed history of the region, and fortunately it was written in English. Tracey's fluency in Italian was something that Moira had not considered. To have found the book but not been able to understand it would have been frustrating. Page 25 seemed to have nothing to do with the castello, and Moira was ready to close the book in disgust when she read the last paragraph:

"The Nazi war criminal, Helmut Kauffman, is believed to have escaped to South America. (See ilus., p. 222)"

This must be what Tracey had discovered — nothing to do with Elspeth at all. She had been looking for Helmut Kauffman, the German colonel who had taken over the castello, Sergio's father. Hastily turning the pages to a group of illustrations, Moira found page 222. There were shots of bomb devastation and groups of soldiers, but nothing about Helmut Kauffman. Then to her shock she saw it: a picture of a fat man in German uniform, his many chins sunk in his high military collar, the small piggy eyes peering out from folds of flesh. Moira caught her breath, her hands growing so clammy that she almost dropped the book. Helmut Kauffman was Mr. Bear.

With shaking hands she returned the book to the shelf. Now one of those voices that she had found familiar last night left no doubt as to its identity. Mr. Bear had not left the hotel, as she had thought, but merely gone underground in the private apartments.

Glancing around to make sure no one was about, Moira went inside the private office; but though she searched everywhere, no key was to be found. Wondering if she should take her discovery to the police, Moira slithered against the wide stone windowsill. The mechanism of the closed blind was released by her elbow, and yelping in surprise, she drew back from the sill as the blind snapped into place with a sound like a gunshot.

Smiling at the incident, Moira picked herself up. In her haste she had overturned a potted plant, spilling soil onto the polished floor. The poor thing would probably never flower again, she thought guiltily as she crammed the roots inside the terra-cotta pot. Something hard, wrapped in plastic, at the bottom of the pot grazed her fingers. Moira fished it out, and before she had shaken the packet free of the clinging earth she recognized Elspeth's cross. Carlo must have hidden it in his office!

Hardly able to open the plastic in her excitement, Moira took out the jewelry, turning it over to learn at last what he had seen on its reverse side. All she found were two long numbers. They were freshly engraved, for the cross had been fashioned long before serial numbers came into use. On a hunch Moira withdrew Tracey's book from her purse and compared the numbers on the flyleaf. They matched. Whatever significance those phone numbers had, Moira was determined to follow the lead herself. The Fiori chief of police had been so sure that there was no connection between Elspeth's death and this cross, but now she was convinced otherwise, her theory strengthened by the added evidence in Tracey's book. Of course, Emilio Letti knew nothing about that, and Moira was going to make sure he did not find out.

Moving as rapidly and quietly as she could, she made her way back to the public rooms, several times narrowly missing discovery as the servants resumed their household chores.

Safe at last, she hurried upstairs, clutching her purse, conscious of the paperback and her priceless find tucked innocently beneath the white crocheted fabric. If only they knew, she thought, taking the stairs two at a time — whoever *they* were.

"Hi, you're in a hurry," Chris greeted, meeting her outside her door.

"Oh, I was looking for something," she mumbled, guilt over her secret flushing her cheeks.

"What is it? You sure look weird. Are you all right?"

Glad of his strength to lean on, Moira

clutched his arm, encouraged by the warm substance of reality beneath his pink-striped sleeve. "Can we sit down?"

"Sure." He led her to a stone bench beneath the window on the landing. "Do you need a drink?"

"No, I'll be all right," she assured him, gripping his arm.

"I've been looking for you. I knew you'd feel rotten when you found out about Tracey," Chris said sympathetically, drawing her face against his shoulder. "Come on, sweetheart, it's okay."

"Tracey was murdered," Moira blurted, clinging to his warm, square hand.

"Come on, now. Murdered? It was an accident," he assured her, patting her shoulder. Then, lowering his voice, he asked, "Wasn't it?"

"No."

"What makes you so sure?"

"Someone tampered with the boat. Tracey was such a strong swimmer that she could have made it to shore. She didn't because she was knocked out," Moira revealed in a hoarse whisper, seeing the surprise on Chris's face.

"The police are capable of finding evidence of foul play, if there's any to be found," he reminded her, his face clearing. "Now, just relax and keep this to yourself, okay?"

"If you think it's best. But she was your friend, too. You've got to admit the whole story seems odd."

"The conte said the launch was being repaired

— that only leaves the rowboat Tracey used. Now, how could someone have followed her?" He laughed, running his hands through his hair as he puzzled over the question.

"Because he lied. I heard the motorboat myself when I was in the garden. I told the police, but they wouldn't believe me. You speak Italian — make them listen," she pleaded, seizing his hand. "I also know why Tracey went to the cypress island."

The expression on Chris's face was hard to interpret. Shock, surprise — but something else — gone so fast that Moira was not sure she had seen it at all.

"You're sure about the launch?"

"Positive."

"I'll tell them, but it probably won't alter anything. They're still pretty feudal around here. The conte's word is gospel. If he says something is so, they automatically believe it. I could tell Sergio."

"No, don't tell him," Moira cried in panic.

"Why not?" Chris asked in surprise. "The conte's hardly his loving brother."

"They're in this together. Don't ask me what the mystery is, because I don't know yet. Just that it includes a million dollars and the contessa's jewels. It's so complicated I don't know where to begin."

Two maids appeared around the corner, bundles of sheets and pillowcases clutched in their strong, brown peasant arms.

"Sit tight, don't tell a soul," Chris urged, allowing them to pass.

In a moment he was gone, leaving Moira to review the implications of what she had revealed. At least now she was not alone with her dangerous knowledge. Chris was her friend: the only one she had.

Chapter 10

When no contact with the police had been made by evening, Moira began to wonder if Chris had convinced them after all. Were they still so in awe of *Il Conte* that they would not accept the truth? A girl was dead because of him — Perhaps two, she added uneasily, thinking about Elspeth. To acknowledge those suspicions made Moira shudder. More than anything else she had wanted Carlo to be innocent of any crime; for though she fought against it, part of her loved him still.

If there were still no word by morning, she would demand to see the police. Abruptly she turned her back on the velvet-blue sky, hating the mocking reminder of that first evening with Carlo, the memory stirred by the fragrance of the night-blooming flowers on the terrace. She would take the sports car into town. If she went early, Carlo would still be asleep, tired after this evening's festivities. Loud dance music vibrated from the banqueting hall, growing more frenetic as the hours passed. Carlo usually stayed till the dance was over, his presence adding that high-toned flavor of the aristocracy, which was such an integral part of the celebration.

She might be caught, Moira considered as she

walked upstairs, forcing her eyes away from the magnetic pull of the noisy throng in the brightly lit hall. But on the other hand, she might not. "In for a penny, in for a pound," as Elspeth would have said.

Fortunately the man in the garage was not Maffeo. Acting as if this were a daily occurrence, though her hands shook at the thought of discovery, Moira told him the car number. He brought the car with no questions asked. This in itself made her uneasy. Surely Carlo would have given instructions not to let her use the car now that she was close to discovering his involvement in the crime. Or did she only *think* that this journey was being undertaken without his knowledge? Carlo could be far cleverer than she gave him credit for.

It was fragrant in the early morning hours, and she would have enjoyed the drive had it not been for the nagging fear behind her visit. To her dismay the police station was shuttered. A local boy, who appeared to understand English, pointed toward the harbor, laughingly calling something as he raced away.

In annoyance Moira got back into the car, deciding to try Emilio Letti one last time. If necessary she would even tell him about the phone numbers in Tracey's book, in the hope that the police would have more luck than she when she asked the operator to locate them. She started the engine, lurching the spirited car toward the crossroads, thinking about what the boy had shouted. *Pesce* meant fish; she remembered the word from the hotel menu. The incompetent must have closed up shop to go fishing, she fumed, understanding the boy's laughter. She pushed her foot to the floor, recklessly enjoying the surge of speed.

On the journey Moira wondered if Carlo were following, though she saw no pursuing car in the rearview mirror. Had he allowed her to take the car in an effort to trap her? When Moira recalled how romantic she had felt about him at the beginning of her vacation, she could have wept. If she had been wise, she would have known that everything was too perfect. That shattering day on the island when he had discovered that she was related to Elspeth and even her suspicions generated by the hidden cross had not destroyed all her dreams. The eye-opener had been that careless note to Tracey — and the sound of the motor launch purring through the night. Those two things made her more afraid of him than any other discovery she had made.

Emilio Letti was not in his office, and his assistant was unenthusiastic about contacting him. Thwarted once more, Moira walked outside in the cool morning air, conscious of the noise as the town came to life. She paused to admire the attractive view across the valley, wishing she had remembered her camera, though tourist equipment had seemed out of place on so important a mission.

An attractive stucco mansion, which Moira

decided was either a hotel or the home of local nobility, caught her eye. She sat on the low wall outside a store, wondering what to do till the chief of police arrived. For want of something better to fill her time, she went inside and bought two picture postcards of the town. Returning to her seat on the wall, Moira addressed one to her parents and the other to Jenny at the tobacconist's. Guiltily she counted the days since she had written to either of them. First the excitement of dating Carlo, then the thickening mystery surrounding Elspeth had taken most of her time.

While she purchased stamps for her postcards, Moira asked the apple-cheeked shopkeeper about the large house on the mountain. Though the woman understood English, her reply was heavily accented. With difficulty Moira finally grasped what she was saying.

"A sanitarium," she voiced with surprise. What a shame! A visit to a local tourist spot would have passed the time.

"*Si*, many doctors there. People come all over, be better," the woman managed, beaming at her accomplishment.

"Well, I hope I don't need their services," Moira remarked grimly as she counted her change. "Is there anything else to see? I'm waiting for someone, and I've got a little time to kill."

Struggling with the sentences, the woman laughed at her words. "To kill — that strange way to say, signorina. No, only the convent. Sisters help the good doctors with their miracles. Tourists come sometime — see building, very old."

Moira thanked the woman for her help. It would pass time to look at it, though her memories of convents were not pleasant; they held too many reminders of Elspeth. Lately the nagging memory of her cousin shadowed each day with an uncanny obstinacy. A drive through pleasant mountain scenery on a sight-seeing tour might take her mind off the disturbing events at Hotel Castello.

After she crossed the green, fertile valley, the uphill journey was so steep that Moira decided to park the car and continue on foot. It was as if she were alone in the mountains. Only a few goats cropping vegetation behind crumbling stone walls kept her company. At last the first summit was reached, and Moira sat down to rest. To her surprise she saw a drinking fountain set in the rock wall of a roadside shrine, and she thankfully slaked her thirst, revived by the icy spring. Before a gilded figure of the Madonna burned a small, red-glass oil lamp, and the feet of the statue were buried beneath a carpet of bright summer flowers.

Voices sounded through the trees behind the shrine, and Moira realized that it stood at the entrance to a house. While she wondered if she had reached the sanitarium or the convent, three dark-robed figures appeared from the massed wall of beech and chestnut trees. Nodding politely to her, the first nun knelt briefly before the shrine. Then, blessing herself, she moved toward the ever narrowing road uphill.

This sudden appearance of the nuns turned Moira's composure to alarm. It was an idiotic reaction, yet she could not stifle the surge of unease that gripped her. It must be the unexpected reminder of school while Elspeth's memory was still so real, she consoled herself, forcing composure as she admired the distant clustered buildings of Fiori. From here they were almost alpine in appearance. There were many flowers, though they were not the riotous explosion of color she had seen in Santa Maria, the miles north changing this mountainside to a quieter, more serious land.

"You have car trouble, signorina?"

At the unexpected voice Moira leaped in alarm, relieved to find that it was only an elderly nun who wanted to help.

"You surprised me," she apologized in embarrassment, seeing concern at her reaction in the sister's wrinkled face.

"Are you ill?"

"No. My car is parked down there. I'm really all right."

At her insistence the nun smiled and nodded, moving surefootedly over the rugged terrain. With a friendly wave the second nun followed her companion. Moira gradually became aware of her shaking hands, and she clasped them firmly in her lap as she watched the women toil slowly uphill, two dark shapes etched against the greenery. Turning back to the shrine, Moira was alarmed to find the third nun standing within inches of her, her black habit shutting out the sunlight, blackening the warm stone seat with a tall, sinister shadow.

Afterward Moira could not be sure what had really happened. It was like a nightmare. She remembered looking up at the black-robed figure, noticing something startlingly familiar about the way the woman moved. Then, a single red carnation, taken from the shrine, was dropped in her lap.

Holding the spicy flower, Moira heard a familiar voice echoing through a wave of paralyzing shock: "Hello, Moira."

Then the woman was gone, swiftly covering the ground as she moved toward the cover of the trees.

Moira was stunned. It was several moments before she gathered her wits sufficiently to call, "Elspeth!"

The woman walked doggedly forward, ignoring her cry. Leaping to her feet, Moira ran after them until she fell, skinning her knees on the rocky ground. It was useless to follow. They had already disappeared through the trees, where she could see a large stone building, slate-colored against the leaves. Cradling her bleeding knees, Moira laid her head against her arms, and crouched on the dusty ground, she began to sob.

After a few minutes she felt better, the release of emotion soothing the shock that gripped her. It had been just a glimpse, after all; she could not be sure, she told herself. Lately she had become obsessed by Elspeth's memory. Could that obsession have played on her mind to such an extent that she was hallucinating? This was a practical solution, for those women were definitely flesh and blood; there was nothing ghostly about the sister who had inquired about her welfare or the young one who had joined her companion on the rocky path. It was only the third sister who had struck fear through Moira's heart. A glimpse of that shadowed face had sent her blood pounding with shock. Impossible as it seemed, Moira was convinced that she had seen Elspeth's face beneath the concealing habit.

Picking herself up and trying to dust away the powdery rock that clung to her stockings, Moira winced at her stinging wounds. At the spring she bathed her knees, wadding her handkerchief into a makeshift bandage. It was then that she noticed the dusty flower trampled on the ground. However successfully she convinced herself that it had been a hallucination, this flower was real. And the significance of the carnation only added credence to the event. Red carnations had been Elspeth's fashion trademark. Only she would have chosen this from amongst the flowers at the shrine. There was also the voice, which had spoken her name. Who but Elspeth could have known it?

After patching her wounds and washing her

face in the chilling spring water, Moira began the downhill trek. Fear was gradually replaced by clear reasoning as she drove back to Fiori, reconstructing the details of this frightening encounter.

By the time she met Emilio Letti in the cafe by the museum, much of Moira's assurance about their meeting had evaporated. He was a dark, dapper little man with eyes forever roving. Today he wore a pale shantung suit and wide-brimmed white hat. As she had expected, he smilingly dispatched her latest scare with the suggestion that perhaps the sun was stronger than she had realized.

"To someone from another climate our weather can be treacherous at this time of year, even in the mountains," he suggested, ordering her a cool drink. "Of course, my dear signorina, what you have suggested is preposterous. But the sheer foolishness of your theories always fascinates me."

Put out by his open amusement, Moira sipped her drink. Let him laugh, she thought in annoyance, watching his chiseled face, turned in profile toward the door. "I'm sorry to have wasted your time."

"Not at all." He smiled, patting her arm. "In fact you've proved a pleasant diversion to an otherwise boring day."

"Look, Signor Letti, I had no intention of providing a diversion. I came to you for help, not to be laughed at."

"And help you shall receive. When I have any further news, dear signorina, I promise to let you know."

"It wasn't the sun. I know I saw her. Don't you realize what I'm saying? My cousin is *alive*," Moira insisted.

Emilio Letti patted her arm. "Yes, I know you believe that. But last week you came to me equally convinced that your cousin had been the victim of a bizarre murder plot involving one of the noblest families in Northern Italy."

When he presented her behavior in that light, it did seem irrational. Last week she had been so positive that Elspeth had been murdered, while today she was no longer sure.

"I suggest that you go back to the castello and enjoy the remainder of your holiday. Surely an attractive lady like you can find more interesting diversions than amateur detecting."

She bit her lip to keep back her words of indignation. As she had suspected in the beginning, Emilio Letti was probably up to his neck in the mystery. Or it could be that he had never taken her seriously after all. His refusing to take her word against Carlo's concerning the boat should have been convincing enough. What more did she need? Still, she could play along with his theory in order to take him off guard.

"The motives for killing Elspeth are clear," she began confidently. "Sergio was jilted and Bettina Corri wanted to be Campella's leading girl."

He smiled in his amused, indulgent manner and continued to drink his espresso.

"Well?" she prompted impatiently.

"I wonder why we need a police force at all with such efficient help."

"With less than a week before I go home, I thought you could profit from my assistance," Moira snapped.

"That was kind of you. It's just that your assistance, however well-intentioned, is more likely to hamper police efforts than help them. I do hope you are not offended."

She was more than offended. Living on nerves, as she had done these past few days, left Moira only a thin line of patience, one that snapped under his patronizing air. Her usually dormant temper was roused, and unable to contain herself, she exploded. "Is that so? Without me you wouldn't *have* a case to investigate! I was the one who told you about the cross in the first place!" Blood colored her fair skin until her face glowed, and Moira gulped the last of her drink in an effort to quench the fire.

"Correct, dear signorina, but now that we do have a case, I urge you not to interfere. Such ineptitude could warn the culprit." The fixed smile, which he had maintained throughout their meeting, faded, setting his pencil-thin moustache in a black line. "In fact I order you to stop at once. This cross to which you attach such importance, the lady to whom you lay such blame — these things are meaningless."

"How can you say that?" Moira exploded, the temptation to prove him wrong almost conquering her good sense. What would he say when she presented the cross and the book to prove her point?

Glancing about the restaurant to make sure they were not overheard, Emilio Letti lowered his voice. "There are a number of things you don't know about this case. For one, your cousin's life was heavily insured. When so much money is involved, there is usually an investigation before any claims are settled. We've been aware of the situation for some time, the possibility that your cousin's accident was a well-planned murder."

Moira's mouth dropped open in surprise at his revelation. "Someone killed her for money?"

"At first it appeared that way. Now we are no longer sure. I can tell you no more, beyond the fact that Bettina Corri was safely in Switzerland at the time of the accident. As for being jilted" — here he smiled, amused by her theory — "dear lady, men are often placed in that position, and they do not murder because of it, romantic though it might seem. Even the conte, whom you consider as Sergio's replacement, suffered the same fate. Does that set your mind at rest?"

The result was to the contrary. Long after Moira had left the police chief to his paperwork, her mind somersaulted from one conclusion to another. Who was the beneficiary in Elspeth's policy? She had been too stunned to ask. He purposely had mentioned no names, which was his way of saying that it was none of her business. But it *was* her business. Elspeth had been her cousin.

Long before Moira reached the shadowy walls of Santa Maria, grown mellow in the afternoon sun, a frightening idea seized her, one so unpleasant that she wanted to reject it. Who needed money so desperately that he might kill to obtain it? There was only one person fitting that description: Carlo. It was not just Tracey's life in question, but Elspeth's, too — yet who was that woman on the mountain?

On the twisting drive to Santa Maria, the car seemed to have a will of its own. Moira was not sure whether it was her inattention or if there were actually something wrong with the steering. Several times, without warning, the car pulled toward the edge of the road, almost running onto the narrow shoulder that was the only barrier between safety and the terrifying drop over the mountainside. Her hands shook as she gripped the wheel, her head pounding with tension and fear. Was she losing her mind? First imagining the nun to be Elspeth and now almost compulsively steering over the mountainside.

Glad to be in the safety of the hotel, Moira left a message for the garage about the car's steering. The lobby was bare without the Campella people. There were no wicker hampers or theatrical props, no beautifully made-up girls draped languidly on the green upholstered hotel chairs.

Only a handful of visitors remained, and the hotel staff appeared to be tired and bored. The realization that in a few days she, too, would be leaving shook Moira from her mental confusion. Little time remained to solve the chain of events that stayed outside her grasp. At first she had uncovered too many suspects, but now that problem had been solved. Only Carlo was left. And she had four days to discover the truth.

Chapter 11

On Thursday morning Moira was awakened by a knock on her door, and she shuddered with apprehension when she heard Carlo announce breakfast. Her pulse quickening with mingled emotions, she slipped on her robe before answering the door.

Dressed in a bright-yellow silk shirt, the color contrasting magnificently with his tan, he stood on the threshold holding her breakfast tray.

"Buon giorno," he greeted.

"Buon giorno," Moira repeated stiffly, wondering why this sudden interest in her welfare, unless he was closing in for the kill. The frightening thought made her shudder.

"You're cold. Go back to bed," he ordered, coming inside the room and closing the door. When he saw disapproval in her face, Carlo laughingly promised, "You have my word that I shall act like a gentleman." He drew back the curtains with a swish.

Then, lounging in her white satin chair, he propped his feet on the edge of the dressing table and waited.

"You surprised me," Moira said as she crumbled a roll onto her plate, regaining some of her composure. Had he seen the spilled soil from that plant pot and discovered her theft?

"Don't be too surprised to eat," he said, glancing over the array of toilet articles on the dressing table.

When she was finished Moira put the tray aside and waited for him to speak. Carlo lay back, eyes closed, and only when she cleared her throat to get his attention did he open them.

"Finished?"

"Yes. What do you want?"

He frowned at her bluntness. "I want to know why you told them you heard the launch?"

Moira stiffened at the question, dropping her gaze from the piercing intensity of his brown eyes as Carlo leaned forward in the chair, awaiting her answer.

"It was the truth. I did hear it."

"But Maffeo told them the boat had a leak."

"I'm sure Maffeo told them only what you allowed," Moira snapped, boldly facing the anger in his face.

"The man has a tongue of his own" was Carlo's swift retort as he leaped to his feet. He paused in the doorway, his hand on the knob. "By the way, the car is not available to you any more."

"I don't need it now," she snapped. "Thank you."

"The steering is bad. I thought you might like to know."

When he had gone Moira found that she was shaking with a mixture of fear and anger. Why had he told her the car had faulty steering if he had been the one who had tampered with it?

Maybe it was a mechanical defect after all.

Wondering if her room had been ransacked yesterday while she was out, Moira found the cross and the useless phone numbers where she had left them. Though she re-examined it, the novel presented no further clues. Now she regretted mentioning either the nun or Mr. Bear's real identity to Emilio Letti. He would probably convey this news to Carlo before long, if he had not already done so. Was that what had prompted Carlo's solicitous morning visit?

Several times during the day Moira tried to speak to Chris, but she was told that he was out. After dinner Moira left the terrace, where the air was still and heavy with an impending thunderstorm. Beneath the door to her room she found a note, and thinking it was from Chris, she opened it, her mouth going dry when she read a message identical to the one Tracey had received the day she was killed. After a moment's consideration Moira decided to take Carlo up on the invitation; but she would use the launch herself. First, however, she would leave Chris a note, telling him to call the police and bring them to the island.

In the darkness the ruins seemed larger and more ghostly than she remembered. Shivering at the foreboding appearance of the island villa, Moira guided the boat toward the jetty, carefully avoiding the grotesque cypress trunks, conscious of the choppy water, whipped by a steadily rising wind. When Carlo had shown her how to operate the boat she had not realized that she would ever be taking it out by herself.

It was comforting to recall the message she had slipped beneath Chris's door, her insurance against danger. Any time now he would be reading her scribbled words and calling the police.

Beaching the boat, she sloshed through the shallows, shivering as the wind picked up, rippling the water to a swelling wave. Thunder rumbled nearer, while over the mountains livid flashes of lightning ripped the sky in two.

Carlo had not told her where to meet him, and Moira's heart quickened with fear as she climbed the steep terraced steps. Too late did she review the possibility that Chris might not go to his room after dinner. The more she dwelled on the idea, the more terror-stricken she became. All her confidence evaporated at the realization that she could only be sure that two people knew of this meeting: Carlo and herself. The thought made her knees knock, and she forced herself to walk faster, trying to thrust fear to the back of her mind. She had come this far — there was no turning back.

As she walked toward the bushes, a shadow moved beside the arbor. It was too gloomy to distinguish much between lightning flashes. Footsteps were masked by the fierce wind gusting from the lake, whipping tree branches in a noisy barrage. Moira called his name, but the wind blew her voice away. Huge raindrops suddenly spattered against her face, and clutching her stole about her hair, Moira dashed for the shelter of the arbor.

To her surprise no one was there. Uneasily Moira recalled these legends of an evil presence who lured others to the waters of the lake. Had she only imagined a man's shadow beside the arbor? Was it something more terrifying that awaited her in the storm? The shriek of the wind would drown any cries. Even if screams were heard, the superstitious servants would attribute the voice to the spirit of the lake, and fearfully crossing themselves, they would shutter the windows against demons.

There was a shadow. This time she was not mistaken. Someone moved out from the rhododendron bushes against the wall, a black shape, wide-shouldered, tall enough for a man.

"Carlo," she called again, her voice smothered by the wind.

A movement from the steps to the beach took Moira's attention, and she tried to distinguish the identity of her mysterious visitor as a sheet of lightning blazed across the garden.

A scream escaped her lips as heavy footsteps sounded behind her and someone gripped her shoulders. With racing heart Moira turned in the light embrace. "Carlo?"

But the figure suddenly thrust into bright relief against the vine-tangled wall was Chris.

"Sorry to disappoint you." He grinned, his grasp still light. "Some guys have all the luck."

Moira gasped with shock, not knowing whether to be frightened or glad. "What on earth are you doing here?" she demanded, half falling against him, weak with fright.

"That's some kind of greeting! I should be mad." Chris laughed, the sound comforting in the darkness.

"I left a note — you were supposed to call the police," Moira gasped, remembering the message beneath his door.

"Sorry about that." He dismissed it, drawing her to the stone bench running the length of the arbor, where Moira thankfully leaned against the warm comfort of his shoulder.

"What about the conte? He's out there somewhere," she whispered fearfully. "He killed Tracey."

"And knowing that, you were going to meet him tonight. You've got to be nuts!" Chris exclaimed, drawing out of the rain, which lashed in a drenching sheet over the floor.

"But I had it planned. You were supposed to get the police," Moira explained, pulling her knitted stole over her hair to keep it dry. "Anyway, I'm glad you're here."

Chris laughed and drew her close, brushing her forehead with his lips, the warmth of his body taking the chill from her wet arms. The minutes passed until his silence began to play on Moira's nerves, stirring her pangs of fear.

"What's the matter?" she asked, her voice cracking. "Why don't you say something?"

"I feel pretty silly shouting over this wind."

She accepted his reason and was content to watch the storm tearing through the garden, upending flower urns and toppling the gleaming marble figures. Then an alarming thought made her heart skip a beat. If Chris had not received her message, how could he have known that she was coming to the island?

"Chris?"

"What?"

"How did you know about Carlo's note?"

Against her ear she heard his soft laughter, and the sound tightened her scalp, prickling terror along her spine. "Because I sent it."

"You mean, Carlo doesn't know I'm here?"

"That's right."

"But why, silly?"

"It's you who are silly. Do you think you can outwit everyone in your bungling way? Tracey was a smart cookie — at least she was a challenge — but you're a real fruitcake."

Moira's heart stood still, and the pressure of his hands became like lead weights against her throat. With a scream of terror she wrenched free, taking Chris by surprise. Disregarding the pelting rain, she fled from the arbor, stumbling as she ran in a weaving course over the lawns. Rain stung her face while wind-tossed branches lashed sharply against her cheeks, snatching her hair and tearing her clothes. Terror gave wings to her feet, and she sailed through the garden, stumbling over the broken wall to race across the mosaic flooring of the courtyard.

Dark archways loomed before her. Choosing the first one, she plunged forward, the pursuit of the flesh-and-blood man from the garden far more terrifying than any shadowy creature produced by her own imagination. She stumbled down dark passageways, coming out in an upstairs room from where she could see this side of the island. Leaning against the wall to get her breath, Moira heard Sergio's voice blown to her on the wind, his shouts answered a moment later from outside the villa. They were heading this way.

Sobbing and praying, Moira charged from the room, not knowing where the passages went, only knowing that she was going deeper into the ruin. At last, too breathless to go farther, she scrambled up some stairs to find herself in the bell tower. From the campanile she had a perfect view, but there was also no way out. She was trapped.

From the echoing footsteps Moira knew that the men were inside the villa. It was only a matter of time before they found her, and she stifled a sob of defeat. If only Carlo knew she was here. If only she had not trusted Chris so implicitly. His scathing remarks about her being a fruitcake told her that their friendship had not been genuine from the start. And Carlo, whom she loved, had been cloaked in suspicion.

How long she crouched on the debris-littered floor, Moira did not know, too conscious was she of the nearing footsteps as she strained to hear above the wind. Her pursuers were not quiet, but why should they be? All the advantages were theirs.

When the footsteps stopped at the base of the

stairs the wind had almost dropped, the only sound being the steady sweep of rain against the weathered stone walls. Petrified with fear, Moira crouched silently, not daring to breathe, not answering when a voice hailed her from below.

"Get out of the way. I'll get her."

That was Chris. Moira could not mistake his voice, though now the friendly warmth had gone, replaced by gruff determination. In a moment he was beside her, his eyes gleaming in the light beamed upstairs by his companion.

"Why run?" was all he asked as he grabbed her arms, dragging her toward the head of the narrow, open stairs.

"Go on. You got up — you can get down."

Sobbing as she made the treacherous descent, made doubly precarious by Chris's impatient hustling from behind, Moira reached the room below. A lantern rested on a slab of rock where the conspirators huddled, miserable in their soaked clothing. There was Sergio, of course, but the identity of the other men came as an unpleasant shock: Maffeo and Mr. Bear. Gasping as the fat one lunged toward her, Moira tried to pull free of Chris's arm, but she could not break his grip.

"Well, well, Miss Connor, what a pity to have to kill you," Mr. Bear said, rolling toward her. She almost retched as his flaccid hand stroked her hair and face. "So pretty."

"Come on, come on," Chris snapped impatiently, but he was silenced by the flash of anger on the German's face.

"Where's the money?" Sergio demanded, his voice tremoring, his face so taut that Moira could see he was close to the breaking point.

Mr. Bear took him aside, gently but with determination. After a hurried conference in Italian Mr. Bear resumed his post, leering at Moira, only inches from her face.

"Now, seeing as you must be the one she gave them to, we want those account numbers."

Moira's mind was blank; then the penciled numbers in the book came into focus. "They're in the book," she whispered.

"What book?"

"One she gave me . . . I threw it away," Moira cried, seizing a chance for freedom.

"Where did you throw it?" Mr. Bear demanded, his breath hitting her face in short, impatient puffs.

"In the wastebasket in my room."

"She's lying," Chris said impatiently.

"I bet she gave it to Carlo," Sergio hissed, his eyes gleaming metallic in the light. "Is that where it is?"

"He doesn't know. Nobody knows. I thought they were phone numbers," Moira whispered, afraid of the madness in Sergio's eyes as he caught her wrist.

Mr. Bear threw back his head and laughed, his bellow echoing through the empty villa. "Phone numbers! That's very funny! My dear lady, those numbers represent a very fat Swiss bank account. Come now, don't say you didn't know?" he wheedled, taking Sergio's hand from her. "Your cousin double-crossed us. *You* aren't going to be that foolish, are you?"

"No," Moira whispered, shrinking from the expression in his eyes. "I've told you where it is."

While they discussed their next move, Moira was left under Maffeo's surveillance. He seemed embarrassed to be caught in such a compromising situation, but when she begged him to let her escape, the garageman shook his head, glancing furtively toward his employers in case they had heard.

To be on the safe side, Mr. Bear decided that someone would return to the hotel and get the book before disposing of her. And if she had any ideas of escape, they were squashed when he elected to help Maffeo guard her.

When the other two men had gone, Maffeo suggested, since it was cold and drafty in this room, that they should go to a lower level, where he knew of a fireplace where they could light a fire to dry their clothes. Mr. Bear jumped at the idea, heartily disliking his soggy jacket and shoes.

With Moira between them the men went down the narrow stairs to the ground floor, and though she watched for an opportunity to escape, none arose. Soon a roaring fire was burning in the hearth, fed by dry wood from broken doors and furniture heaped against the far wall. The men draped their coats on makeshift airers made from broken chair backs and sat around the blaze drying their shoes.

A cry from beyond the villa broke through the scene of almost domestic tranquillity, and Maffeo's eyes rolled in terror at the inhuman wail. With muttered prayers he crossed himself, casting around among the gloomy shadows of the room for the unseen presence.

With a stifled oath Mr. Bear marched toward the window and leaned out, shouting a warning to whoever was there. In a flash Moira took advantage of the situation. While Maffeo muttered his Ave's for deliverance and Mr. Bear angrily challenged the presence, Moira darted for the door leading to the mosaic courtyard. She was barely through when Mr. Bear yelled for Maffeo to follow. Racing as fast as she could, Moira fled toward the garden, with Maffeo and Mr. Bear in hot pursuit.

Veering away from the beach, she charged through the the garden to the other side of the island. Though taking a chance on the terrain, Moira guessed that neither of the men would have any more advantage in the wet, tangled undergrowth. Mr. Bear, puffing and blowing, lagged far behind, while Maffeo, who was still praying, gained steadily on her.

It was too soon after her exertion for Moira to run as fast as she wanted, and in terror she darted from a screen of bushes, heading for a ramshackle building that looked like a deserted boathouse. With any luck they would think she was still in the garden, she thought, painfully drawing her breath through lungs that felt as if they were on fire.

In the shadow of the building she threw herself against the wall, watching Maffeo clear the bushes on the rise of ground. He scanned the deserted stretch of beach, waiting for the corpulent Mr. Bear to join him; then, as Moira prayed they would, they plunged back into the shrubbery.

For the moment she was safe. It was a wonderful feeling. With gulping breaths Moira slid to the ground, conscious of her bursting lungs, too tired even for thought. Her head against her knees, she stiffened in terror to feel a soothing hand laid gently on her hair — a woman's hand.

Stifling a cry, Moira leaped to her feet, surprised by the speed of her reaction. A tall, black shadow loomed from the darkness, white hands outstretched. Moira backed against the wall, but the figure came on. In cold horror she recognized a nun's habit.

Moira tried to run, but the woman cut off her escape. From the blackness of the rainswept night a voice, tinged with the soft brogue of Castle Brennan, reproached her. "Now, Moira, why are you afraid of me?"

Moira fainted.

When she regained consciousness she was lying on the floor of the boathouse, a figure bending over her — but it was sharply defined, with no soft, concealing folds.

"Are you all right? *Dio!* I thought . . ." Carlo caught her against him, cradling her head on his shoulder as she wept.

"Please, signorina, could you be more quiet?"

Moira recognized the polite voice of Emilio Letti, who came from the shadows, his finger against his lips. "Please."

"How did you know?" she sobbed, trying to stifle her choking shudders against Carlo's shirt.

"We found the note you left for Signor Bern. Why didn't you tell me everything, *cara?* You were always too busy suspecting me." Carlo stopped as Emilio Letti signaled to him for silence.

Shouts came from the distance, and Moira recognized Mr. Bear's grating voice. Now she saw him staggering after Maffeo, who was racing over the beach toward the boathouse.

"Are they armed?" Emilio Letti demanded.

"I don't know."

"We'll have to take the chance," he decided, squashing Carlo's angry objection. "Draw them down here."

Moira hesitated, remembering that ghostly figure who had loomed from the shadows. "I . . . I can't, please."

"You must," Emilio Letti commanded, pushing her in his urgency, as she stumbled to her feet. "Hurry!"

As she sidled around the building Moira became aware of a boat beached behind the shed, and there were other people crouched there, waiting. Of course! Carlo had led the police down the private road to the jetty on the far side of the island, an escape that Moira had forgotten existed. With shaking legs she walked into view, expecting to see the apparition, but to her relief there was nothing but sand.

"There she is!" Maffeo shouted in excitement.

"We have you now. And you'd better talk! That book wasn't in your room," Mr. Bear bellowed, his voice cracking as he gulped for breath.

"It's not in the trash. It's in my drawer," she called, praying that the police would provide cover if shots were exchanged.

Maffeo reached her as two men appeared from the shrubbery. Chris and Sergio streaked down the beach to join their companions, forming a threatening circle around her.

"All right, sweetheart, we want the truth this time," Chris growled, reaching for her throat.

"Madre di Dio!" Maffeo screamed, cowering against the building.

That same ghostly, dark-habited figure appeared, gliding along the shoreline. Moira followed the men's startled gaze until Sergio broke free, shouting at the top of his voice as he charged toward the apparition.

Now the waiting policemen spilled from behind the boathouse, quickly fanning across the expanse of beach as the criminals darted for cover. The chase was brief.

An hour later Moira watched the sunrise from the dining room in the private apartments of Hotel Castello. She was fed and warm, and now the terrifying events of the night receded pleasantly into the past. Concerned about her welfare, Carlo rang for the local doctor to examine her. Though she was pleased by his solicitous action, Moira was bursting with curiosity. She had a million questions to ask both Carlo and Emilio Letti, but neither would answer her inquiries until Doctor Fellini had pronounced her sound, but in need of rest. He left a sedative, though Moira insisted that they explain before she would take it.

Laughingly Carlo agreed, making sure she was comfortably situated on the velvet sofa before he began.

"Last night Signor Letti told me everything, after he went to Bern's room and found your note. For some time we've known that Bern was connected with the American syndicates, and a partner of Herr Kauffman, who operated an Argentinean branch of the business. What I didn't know was Sergio's part in it."

Moira smiled as he took her hand, feeling tired but deliriously happy. "I knew Mr. Bear was Helmut Kauffman. I found his picture in a book in the library."

"So *you* took the cross! I thought it was Bern."

"You found that plant," Moira said guiltily. "I'm sorry."

"What's this talk of plants and bears?" Emilio Letti snorted in disgust, replacing his coffee cup on the table. "I haven't got all day. Begging your pardon, *Signor il Conte*, there's work to be done. You, dear signorina, almost upset a well-laid scheme, on which the police and several insurance-agency detectives had been working for months. The beneficiaries to your cousin's insurance policies were Sergio and a South American businessman named Morales — in reality, Herr Kauffman."

"So he wasn't lying," Moira said in surprise. "He told me he represented a South American firm."

"The firm he represented, dear lady, was no respectable business, but how else could he come to a fashion showing without arousing suspicion? It was the perfect lie to tell."

Remembering his friendliness, Moira asked, "Did he know I was Elspeth's cousin?"

"Oh, yes, they all did."

Moira gasped at the revelation, and Carlo squeezed her hand. "You see, I was the only poor fool taken in by you."

"And Tracey?"

"Signorina Cole worked for the Worldwide Assurance Company, and to give her credit, she almost discovered the entire scheme. I was sorry to lose her," Emilio Letti admitted sadly, picking up his hat and heading for the door.

"But what was the scheme?" Moira demanded, afraid he would leave without telling her the most important part.

"*Il Conte* will tell you that." And he walked outside.

"What does he mean?"

Carlo sighed and went to the window. "You

were right when you thought that I was responsible for your cousin's accident. The contessa's priceless jewels were only paste. I sold the genuine article to an American collector for a fabulous sum."

"Why?"

"It was the only way to keep the castello. Before her death my mother incurred many debts. You've no idea what it costs to outfit a hotel. A friend of Elspeth's offered me money for the privilege of keeping the jewels in his private collection, because, of course, they could never be sold on the open market."

"Now I know why you were so angry when I suggested that you'd moved them."

"I thought you'd discovered my secret. You see, Elspeth was to deposit the money in a Swiss bank. There was nowhere here that I could have banked it without arousing suspicion. What I didn't know was that Bern and Kauffman followed her. Knowing they were on her trail, she panicked and fled without telling me a thing."

"But she had the account numbers put on her cross for you," Moira gasped, realizing now why Elspeth had mutilated the heirloom. "She must have intended to send it to you."

"Probably so, but at the time her intentions didn't help. When she refused to give them the money, Kauffman arranged for her accident. The old cross was stolen from the hotel, and until Bettina wore it I'd forgotten its existence."

"So Alfio lied."

Carlo shrugged. "He did, but he meant no actual harm. Signor Letti has a confession from a maid at the Fiori hotel. The man at the pawnshop thought he was justified in his deception, since the girl desperately needed money."

"When you found out who I was, did you think I knew about your money?"

"Yes," Carlo admitted, "or worse still, that you worked for Kauffman. You sat by him at the show, and you were also friendly with Bern."

Moira grimaced, remembering Mr. Bear's unwelcome attentions.

"When Sergio learned where the money was, he intended to withdraw it with Bettina posing as Elspeth. Of course, when I saw the numbers on the cross I realized what she might have done. I claimed my money, and everything would have ended there if Kauffman hadn't been greedy and stolen the contessa's jewels as a bonus. He must have coveted them all this time."

"Can I ask you something?" Moira began hesitantly. "Did I see a ghost last night, or is Elspeth still alive?"

"It was no ghost."

Her mouth dropped open in surprise. "She's not dead?"

"Elspeth is a sister in the convent of Mary of the Mountain."

The nun she had met on the mountain road was not a hallucination after all, yet it seemed improbable for someone like Elspeth to take the veil.

"But she always loved clothes and night life.

Why did she give it up? And why didn't she let me know she was alive?"

"Though she wasn't killed in the accident, as Kauffman had intended, she was badly scarred. Her career would have been over," Carlo explained sadly.

"How terrible for her."

"Kauffman spirited her away to a sanitarium in the mountains and registered her under a fictitious name. Then he announced her death to the world. When she finally regained consciousness she had amnesia."

"That is why the coffin was so light — it was empty!" Though it was marvelous to know that Elspeth was still alive, Moira was apprehensive about the effect it might have on Carlo's feelings for her. Forcing herself to ask, she whispered, "Do you still love her?"

To her delighted surprise he knelt beside her, taking her in his arms. "I don't think I ever did," Carlo confided huskily. "During those months when I thought she'd stolen the money, I learned to hate her. What I had admired in Elspeth I saw in you, but without her brittleness." With a smile Carlo smoothed her tangled hair from her brow, and Moira kissed his hand.

"You were so natural — the way I thought women had forgotten how to be."

Moira's sigh of relief was so audible that they both burst out laughing. She stretched luxuriously on the couch.

"May I see her?"

Carlo shook his head. "She would rather you didn't, though she'll speak with you. Mother Superior gave her special permission to leave the convent to help you, but she'll return. She's happy there. She feels that her recovery was a miracle, that God brought her back for a life of service."

Moira listened, her eyes misting as she pictured Elspeth, alone and scarred, finding what the sisters at school had given up hope of her ever knowing: faith in God.

"I'll abide by her wishes," she decided, cherishing the memory of her cousin's intervention. "But I wish you'd told me this before. It's lucky I don't have a weak heart."

"Before last night I didn't know about it myself. Only Kauffman knew that she was alive until Tracey alerted the police. I'm glad it's over. All this time I've felt like a criminal."

"Will you have to return the money?"

"No, it's mine. The American has his jewels, and I've got the castello. I told you what sacrifices the del Santa Marias must make to keep their castello."

Moira smiled, and getting up, she found the warm support of his arms comforting. They walked to the window. Servants were setting up striped umbrellas on the terrace for the hotel guests, who would soon begin another day of relaxation.

"You know, this was the most unnerving holiday I've ever spent," Moira confided with feeling.

"I know, and I'm sorry, because your unhappiness was my fault."

Moira grinned at his serious face. "Last night I thought I'd really had it."

"Do you have to go back to work next week? Can't they manage without you?" Carlo whispered, close to her ear, and Moira shivered as his breath tickled her face.

"My parents are expecting me," she said hesitantly.

"We have phones and an excellent mail service," he reminded her, drawing her into his arms. "After all, as owner of the hotel, I'm responsible for your comfort. I insist you spend two weeks at my expense. I won't take 'no' for an answer."

Though she knew she should refuse his offer, Moira did not want to. O'Brien and O'Brien could manage without her, she was sure of that, and Mum and Dad would understand, especially after she told them about Elspeth.

"I'll think about it," she whispered.

"There's one more thing I want you to consider."

"What's that?" she asked, seeing the laughter in his brown eyes.

"Do you think you can prepare to be a contessa in two weeks?" Carlo whispered as he kissed her.

Moira nodded, tears of happiness squeezing beneath her closed lashes. "In two days, darling," she promised.